Interactive Notebook: Life Science

Authors: Schyrlet Cameron and Carolyn Craig

Editor: Mary Dieterich

Proofreaders: Cindy Neisen and Margaret Brown

COPYRIGHT © 2018 Mark Twain Media, Inc.

ISBN 978-1-62223-686-2

Printing No. CD-405009

Mark Twain Media, Inc., Publishers
Distributed by Carson-Dellosa Publishing LLC

Table of Contents

To the Teacher

The *Interactive Notebook* series consists of three books: *Physical Science, Life Science,* and *Earth and Space Science.* The series is designed to allow students to become active participants in their own learning by creating interactive science notebooks (ISN). Each book lays out an easy-to-follow plan for setting up, creating, and maintaining interactive notebooks for the science classroom.

An interactive science notebook is simply a spiral notebook that students use to store and organize important information. It is a culmination of student work throughout the unit of study. Once completed, the notebook becomes the student's own personalized science book and a great resource for reviewing and studying for tests.

The intent of the *Interactive Notebook* series is to help students make sense of new information. Textbooks often present more facts and data than students can process at one time. The books in this series introduce each science concept in an easy-to-read and easy-to-understand format that does not overwhelm the learner. The text presents only the most important information, making it easier for students to comprehend. Vocabulary words are printed in boldfaced type.

Interactive Notebook: Life Science contains 29 lessons that cover three units of study: structure of life, classification of living organisms, and ecological communities. The units can be used in the order presented or in the order that best fits the science curriculum. Teachers can easily differentiate lessons to address the individual learning levels and needs of each student. The lessons are designed to support state and national standards. Each unit consists of two pages.

- **Input page:** essential information for a major science concept, instructions for a hands-on activity, and directions for extending learning
- **Output page:** hands-on activity such as a foldable or graphic organizer to help students process the unit

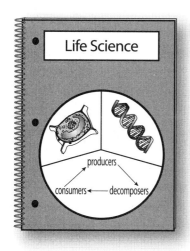
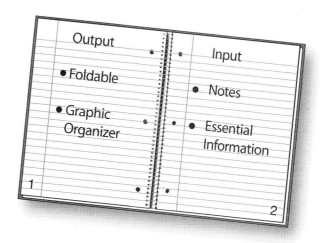

Organizing an Interactive Science Notebook (ISN)

What Is an Interactive Notebook?

Does this sound familiar? "I can't find my homework…class notes …study guide." If so, the interactive science notebook (ISN) is a tool students can use to help manage this problem. An ISN is simply a notebook that students use to record, store, and organize their work. The "interactive" aspect of the notebook comes from the fact that students are working with information in various ways as they fill in the notebook. Once completed, the notebook becomes the student's own personalized study guide and a great resource for reviewing information, reinforcing concepts, and studying for tests.

Materials Needed to Create an ISN

- Notebook (spiral, composition, or binder with loose-leaf paper)
- Glue stick
- Scissors
- Colored pencils (we do not recommend using markers)
- Tabs

Creating an Interactive Science Notebook

A good time to introduce the interactive notebook is at the beginning of a new unit of study. Use the following steps to get started.

Step 1: *Notebook Cover*

Students design a cover to reflect the three units of study (See pages 5 and 6). They should add their names and other important information as directed by the teacher.

Step 2: *Grading Rubric*

Take time to discuss the grading rubric with the students. It is important for each student to understand the expectations for creating the interactive notebook.

Step 3: *Table of Contents*

Students label the first several pages of the notebook "Table of Contents." When completing a new page, they then add its title to the table of contents.

Step 4: *Creating Pages*

The notebook is developed using the dual-page format. The right-hand side is the input page where essential information and notes from readings, videos, or observations, etc., are placed. The left-hand side is the output page reserved for folding activities, diagrams, graphic organizers, etc. Students number the front and back of each page in the bottom outside corner (odd: LEFT-side; even: RIGHT-side).

Step 5: *Tab Units*

Add a tab to the edge of the first page of each unit to make it easy to flip to the unit.

Step 6: *Glossary*

Reserve several pages at the back of the notebook where students can create a glossary of science terms. Students can add an entry for vocabulary words introduced in each unit.

Step 7: *Pocket*

Attach a pocket to the inside of the back cover of the notebook for storage of returned quizzes, class syllabus, and other items that don't seem to belong on pages of the notebook. This can be an envelope, resealable plastic bag, or students can design their own pocket.

Left-Hand and Right-Hand Notebook Pages

Interactive notebooks are usually viewed open like a textbook. This allows the student to view the left-hand page and right-hand page at the same time. You have several options for how to format the two pages. Traditionally, the right-hand page is used as the input or the content part of the lesson. The left-hand page is the student output part of the lesson. This is where the students have an opportunity to show what they have learned in a creative and colorful way. (Color helps the brain remember information better.) The lessons in this book use this format. However, you may prefer to switch the order so that the student output page is on the right and the input page is on the left.

Date: October 22
Standard: Develop model to describe the animal cell structure.
Objective: Identify parts of an animal cell.

Animal Cell

Cell Membrane
Nucleus

Reflection Statement
Cells are very small. They can only be seen with a microscope. Our bodies are made up of millions of cells.

1

Mini-Lesson
The **cell** is the smallest unit of life in all living things. Within a cell are **organelles** (structures); each kind of organelle is specialized to carry out a specific function. Cells work together to help animals perform the activities necessary for life.

Vocabulary
Cell membrane is a thin layer that encloses the cell and controls what materials enter and leave the cell

2

Left-Hand Page   **Right-Hand Page**

The format of the interactive notebook involves both the right-brain and left-brain hemispheres to help students process information. When creating the pages, start with the left-hand page. First, have students date the page, then write the standards and learning objectives to be addressed in the lesson and the essential questions to be answered. Students then move to the right-hand page and the teacher-directed part of the lesson. Finally, students use the information they have learned to complete the left-hand page. The notebook below details different types of items and activities that could be included for each page.

Left-Hand Page Student Output (Odd-numbered pages)	**Right-Hand Page** Input: Teacher-Directed/Content (Even-numbered pages)
• State Standard • Learning Objectives • Essential Questions • Drawings • Diagrams • Illustrations • Graphic Organizers • Reflection Statements • Summaries • Conclusions • Practice Problems • Data from Experiments • Charts and Graphs	• Lecture Notes • Textbook Notes • Study Guides • Video Notes • Mini-Lessons • Handouts • Vocabulary • Lab Notes • Procedures for Experiments • Example Problems • Formulas • Equations

1   2

Interactive Notebook Rubric

Directions: Review the grading rubric below. It lists the criteria that will be used to score your completed notebook. Place this page in your notebook.

Life Science Interactive Notebook Grading Rubric

Category	Excellent (4)	Good Work (3)	Needs Improvement (2)	Incomplete (1)		
Organization	Table of contents and glossary completed. All notebook pages numbered, dated, and titled correctly.	Table of contents and glossary mostly completed. Most pages numbered, dated, and titled correctly.	Table of contents and glossary incomplete. Several pages not numbered, dated, or titled correctly.	Table of contents and/ or glossary missing or incomplete. Little or no attempt to number, date, or title pages correctly.		
Content	All notebook pages completed. All information complete and accurate. All spelling correct.	Most notebook pages completed. One notebook page missing. Most information accurate. Most spelling correct.	Several missing or incomplete notebook pages. Most information inaccurate. Many spelling errors.	Many missing or incomplete notebook pages. Information inaccurate. Little or no attempt at correct spelling.		
Appearance	Notebook pages very neat and organized. Writing and graphics clear and colorful.	Most notebook pages neat and organized. Most writing and graphics clear and colorful.	Notebook pages messy and somewhat disorganized. Writing and graphics messy. Limited use of color to personalize work.	Notebook pages very messy and lack organization. Writing and graphics illegible.		

Student's Comments:

Teacher's Comments:

What Is Life Science?

Mini-Lesson

Read the following information. Then cut out and attach this box to the right-hand page of your science notebook.

Life science is one of several branches of science. It is the study of living organisms. It covers the structure of life, classification of living organisms, and ecological communities. Scientists investigate such topics as cells, plant and animal cycles, genes and heredity, food webs, and biomes.

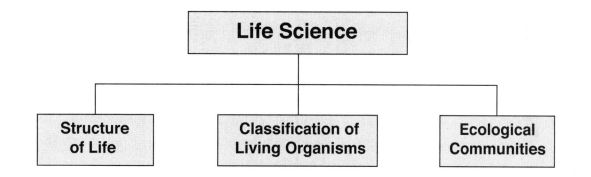

How to Create Your Life Science Notebook Cover

Create a cover that will reflect your study of the three units you will explore in your study of life science.

Step 1: Cut out the title and glue it on the front of your science notebook.

Step 2: Flip through your science textbook to get an idea of the content you will cover as you complete your study of life science.

Step 3: Fill in sections of the circle with colorful drawings and diagrams that reflect the three units of study.

Step 4: Cut out the circle. Apply glue to the back and attach it below the title.

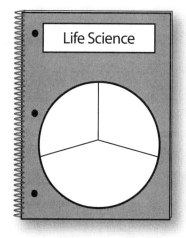

Reflect on What You Have Learned

Write a reflection statement on the left-hand page of your notebook.

Question: What have you learned about life science that you did not know before this lesson? Support your answer with examples and details.

Life Science Notebook Cover

Directions: Create a cover that will reflect your study of the three topics you will explore in your study of life science. Fill in the sections of the template below with colorful drawings and diagrams. Cut out the title and template and glue to the front of your notebook.

Life Science

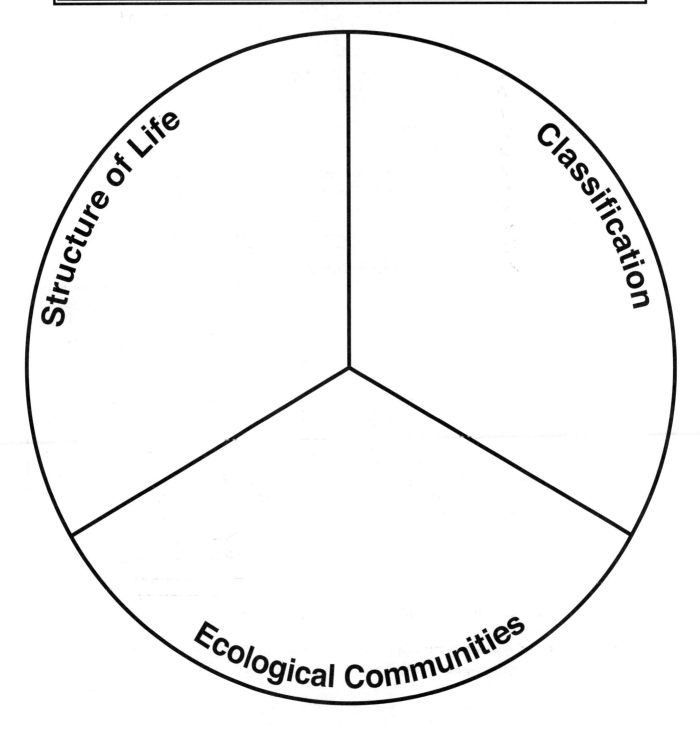

Cells and Types of Cells

Mini-Lesson

Read the following information. Then cut out and attach this box to the right-hand page of your life science notebook. Use what you have learned to create the left-hand page.

All organisms are made up of one or more cells. A **cell** is the basic unit of life. Cells make up living things and carry out the activities that keep living things alive. Cells are living units and are able to make more cells like themselves. New cells can only come from existing cells.

Multicellular organisms are made up of many cells. Snails, fish, trees, and humans are multicellular. The many cells in multicellular organisms are specialized and do only certain jobs. For instance, the root cells of a plant have hair-like projections that absorb water; leaf cells do not have these projections. With specialized cells for different jobs, multicellular organisms can perform more functions than unicellular organisms.

Unicellular organisms are made up of only one cell. Many organisms, including bacteria, are unicellular. The cell of a unicellular organism has structures to help the organism move, get food, reproduce, and respond to its surroundings.

There are basically two main types of cells: eukaryotes and prokaryotes. Cells with a true membrane-bound nucleus are called **eukaryotic cells**. Most cells, including all plants and animals, are eukaryotic, which means that they have all of their nuclear material inside a membrane-bound nucleus. **Prokaryotic cells** do not have a membrane-bound nucleus. They have nuclear material floating around "freely" inside the gel-like cytoplasm but do not have a true nucleus. The simplest cells in existence, bacteria and their relatives, are the only members of this type of cell. Prokaryotic bacteria are little more than a membrane-enclosed container of DNA and other enzymes needed for metabolism and reproduction. The DNA is organized into a single loop that floats inside the cell.

How to Create Your Left-Hand Notebook Page

Complete the following steps to create the left-hand page of your science notebook. Use lots of color.

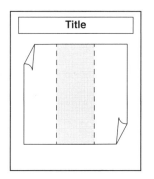

Step 1: Cut out the title and glue it to the top of the notebook page.
Step 2: Cut out the flap chart. Apply glue to the back of the gray tab and attach the chart below the title.
Step 3: Cut out the two picture cards. Glue each card in the correct box on the chart. Write the correct definition under each flap.

Demonstrate What You Have Learned

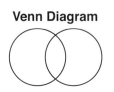

Create a Venn diagram in your life science notebook. Use the diagram to compare and contrast multicellular and unicellular organisms.

Cells and Types of Cells

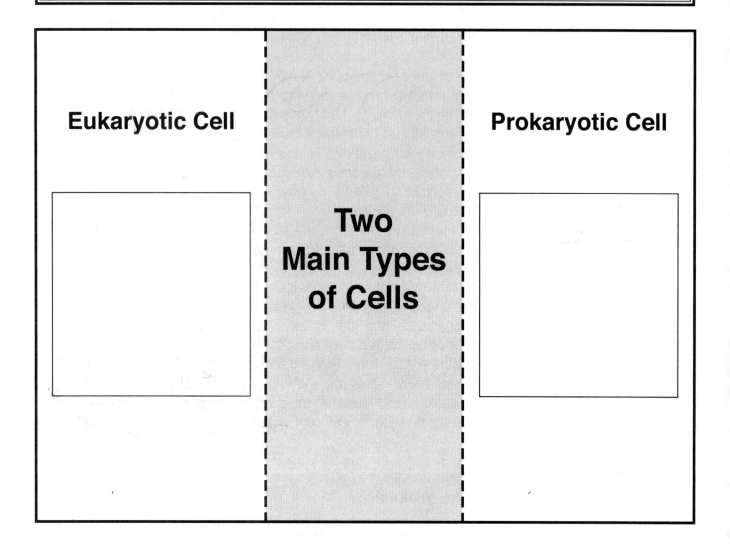

Eukaryotic Cell

Two Main Types of Cells

Prokaryotic Cell

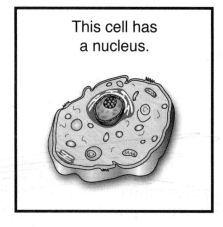

This cell has a nucleus.

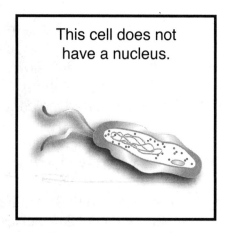

This cell does not have a nucleus.

Diffusion and Osmosis

Mini-Lesson

Read the following information. Then cut out and attach this box to the right-hand page of your life science notebook. Use what you have learned to create the left-hand page.

The cell's membrane has a very important job. The **cell membrane** controls what enters and leaves a cell. The cell needs to maintain its required amounts of water, glucose, and other nutrients, while allowing the elimination of waste. The materials that move into and out of cells are atoms, molecules, and compounds. A **molecule** is the smallest part of a substance that is still that substance. Molecules are made up of tiny parts called *atoms*. Molecules need their space. Molecules are constantly moving from areas where they are more crowded to areas where they are less crowded.

Diffusion is the process where molecules move from crowded areas to less crowded areas. Diffusion in cells keeps all life processes balanced and everything working as it should. In order for a cell to carry on its life processes, oxygen and other substances must pass through the cell membrane, and waste products must be removed from the cell. The membrane has tiny holes in it. Substances can go in and out by moving through the tiny holes. The molecules will continue to move from one area to another until the number of molecules is equal in the two areas. When this occurs, **equilibrium** is reached, and diffusion stops. After equilibrium occurs, it is maintained because molecules continue to move in order to maintain that balance.

Cells contain water and are surrounded by water. **Osmosis** is a special kind of diffusion: it is the diffusion of water through the cell membrane. All chemical reactions in living things take place in water solutions, and most living things use water to transport needed materials throughout their bodies. Water helps to maintain the shape and size of the cell. The water keeps the temperature of the cell constant, which allows life chemical reactions to occur.

How to Create Your Left-Hand Notebook Page

Complete the following steps to create the left-hand page of your life science notebook. Use lots of color.

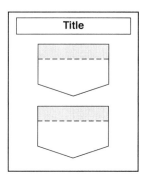

Step 1: Cut out the title and glue it to the top of the notebook page.

Step 2: Cut out the diagram flaps. Apply glue to the back of each gray tab and attach the flaps below the title.

Step 3: Write the correct explanation of the process under each flap.

Demonstrate What You Have Learned

Use a funnel to add a couple of drops of flavoring, such as vanilla, banana, or coconut, to a balloon. After several minutes, smell the balloon. Write an entry in your life science notebook explaining what happened and comparing this activity to diffusion that occurs in cells.

Diffusion and Osmosis

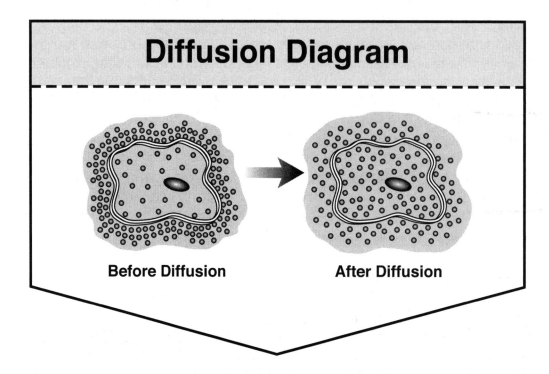

Diffusion Diagram

Before Diffusion   **After Diffusion**

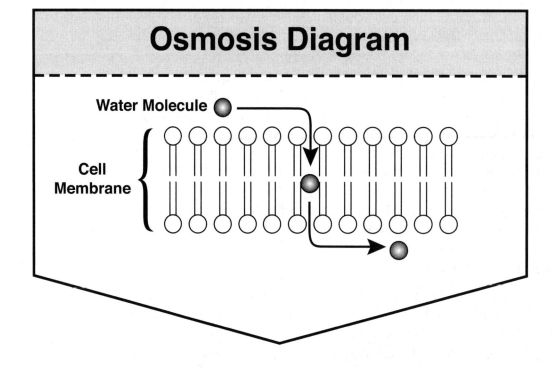

Osmosis Diagram

Water Molecule

Cell Membrane

Cellular Respiration

Mini-Lesson

Read the following information. Then cut out and attach this box to the right-hand page of your life science notebook. Use what you have learned to create the left-hand page.

Cellular respiration is the process in which oxygen is chemically combined with **glucose** (sugar) to produce usable energy for the cell. This process takes place in all living cells. Cellular respiration is a chemical process that can be shown in a chemical equation.

glucose (sugar) + oxygen (O_2) = carbon dioxide (CO_2) + water (H_2O) + energy (as ATP)

Eukaryotic and Prokaryotic Cells

- Animals, plants, fungi, and protists are made up of **eukaryotic cells**. This type of cell contains membrane-bound organelles (cell structures) such as the nucleus and mitochondria. The mitochondria are responsible for producing ATP (adenosine triphospate) for the cell.
- Monerans (bacteria) are **prokaryotic cells** and do not have membrane-bound organelles. Cellular respiration in these organisms occurs in the plasma membrane of the cell.

Glucose used in Cellular Respiration

- Plants, algae, and protists make their own glucose through the photosynthesis process.
- Animals obtain glucose by eating plants.
- Fungi and bacteria absorb glucose as they break down the tissues of plants and animals.

How to Create Your Left-Hand Notebook Page

Complete the following steps to create the left-hand page of your life science notebook. Use lots of color.

Step 1: Cut out the title and glue it to the top of the page.
Step 2: Cut out the flap chart. Apply glue to the back of the gray tab and attach the chart below the title. Write an explanation of the formula under the flap.
Step 3: Cut out the second flap chart. Cut on the solid lines to create two flaps. Apply glue to the back of the gray tab and attach the chart at the bottom of the page. Write the correct explanation under each flap.

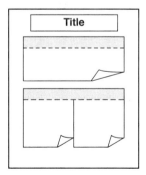

Demonstrate What You Have Learned

When you breathe in, you take in the oxygen your cells need for cellular respiration. When you breathe out, you get rid of the carbon dioxide that your cells produce during cellular respiration. Breathe on a mirror. What did you observe? How is your observation evidence of cellular respiration? Record your answer in your life science notebook.

Cellular Respiration

Chemical Formula for Cellular Respiration

$C_6H_{12}O_6$ + O_2 = CO_2 + H_2O + ATP

Glucose   Oxygen   Carbon   Water   Energy
dioxide

Cellular Respiration

Eukaryotic Cell	Prokaryotic Cell

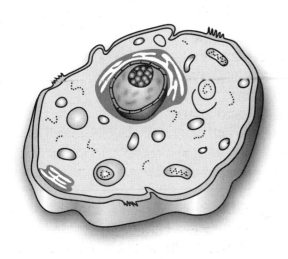

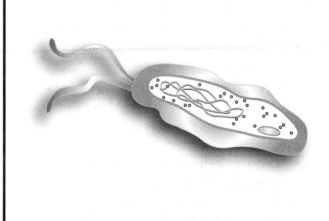

Plant Cell

Mini-Lesson

Read the following information. Then cut out and attach this box to the right-hand page of your life science notebook. Use what you have learned to create the left-hand page.

The cell is the smallest part of any plant. It is the smallest unit that can carry on life processes for a plant. Plants are multicellular organisms with **eukaryotic** (with a nucleus) cells. Their cells work together to help the plants with all of their life functions.

Plant Cell Organelles

- The **cell wall** provides shape and support and protection for the cell. It surrounds the cell membrane.
- The **cell membrane** is a thin layer that encloses the cell and controls what materials enter and leave the cell.
- **Cytoplasm** is the gel-like fluid that fills much of the inside of the cell. It contains proteins, nutrients, and all the other organelles.
- The **nucleus** is the control center of the cell. It is a membrane-bound structure that contains the hereditary material of the cell, the DNA.
- **Chloroplasts** contain the green pigment called chlorophyll that traps light energy and converts it to chemical energy by the process of photosynthesis.
- **Mitochondria** carry out cellular respiration and provide energy to the cells.
- The **vacuole** stores food, water, and waste for the cell.
- The **endoplasmic reticulum** is a network of tubes that transports materials for the cell.
- **Ribosomes** are structures that produce proteins for the cell.
- **Golgi bodies** are structures that package and distribute protein outside the cell.

How to Create Your Left-Hand Notebook Page

Complete the following steps to create the left-hand page of your life science notebook. Use lots of color.

Step 1: Cut out the title and glue it to the top of the notebook page.

Step 2: Cut out the diagram box. Apply glue to the back and attach it below the title.

Step 3: Cut out the 10 vocabulary cards and glue each card in the correct box on the diagram.

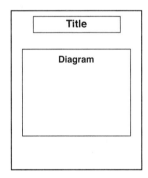

Demonstrate What You Have Learned

Create a three-dimenional plant cell. Line a school milk carton with a sandwich bag. Allow the excess part of the bag to hang over the edges of the carton. Mix lemon gelatin according to the package. Pour the gelatin into the lined carton. When the mixture begins to gel, gently push a variety of candies (gummy worms, jelly beans, and other candies) into the gelatin to represent the organelles of a plant cell. Once the mixture has completely cooled, close the sandwich bag and let set overnight in a refrigerator. Leave the cell in the carton; the carton will represent the cell wall. Create a key identifying the parts of your plant cell.

Plant Cell

Cell Diagram

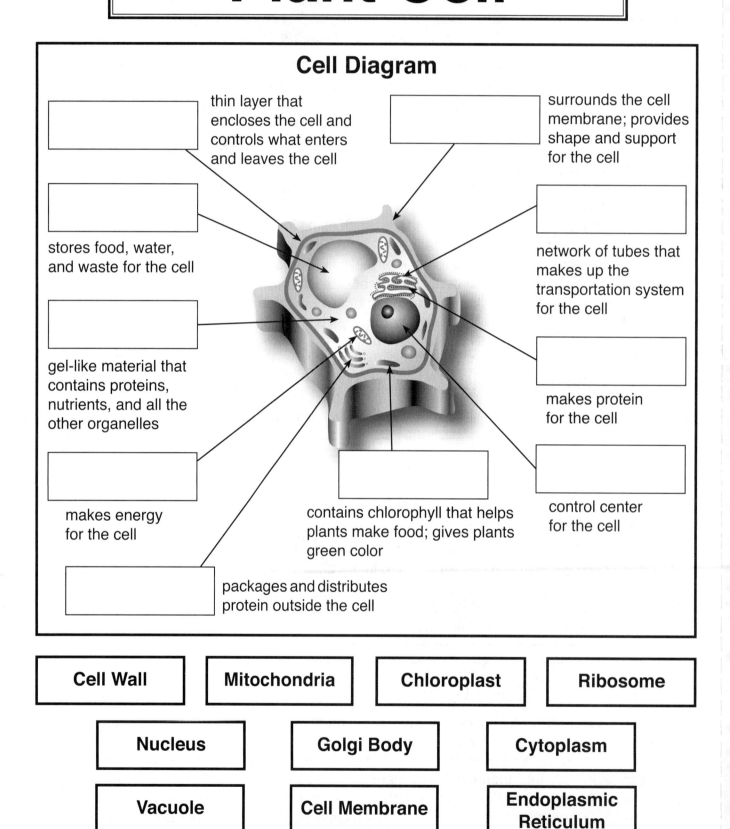

thin layer that enclosts the cell and controls what enters and leaves the cell

surrounds the cell membrane; provides shape and support for the cell

stores food, water, and waste for the cell

network of tubes that makes up the transportation system for the cell

gel-like material that contains proteins, nutrients, and all the other organelles

makes protein for the cell

makes energy for the cell

contains chlorophyll that helps plants make food; gives plants green color

control center for the cell

packages and distributes protein outside the cell

| Cell Wall | Mitochondria | Chloroplast | Ribosome |

| Nucleus | Golgi Body | Cytoplasm |

| Vacuole | Cell Membrane | Endoplasmic Reticulum |

Animal Cell

Mini-Lesson

Read the following information. Then cut out and attach this box to the right-hand page of your life science notebook. Use what you have learned to create the left-hand page.

The cell is the smallest unit of life in all living things. Animals are made up of many different types of cells. Animals are multicellular organisms with **eukaryotic** (with a nucleus) cells. Within a cell are **organelles** (structures); each kind of organelle is specialized to carry out a specific function. Cells work together to help animals perform the activities necessary for life.

Animal Cell Organelles

- The **cell membrane** is a thin layer that encloses the cell and controls what materials enter and leave the cell.
- **Cytoplasm** is the gel-like fluid that fills much of the inside of the cell. It contains proteins, nutrients, and all the other organelles.
- The **nucleus** is the control center of the cell. It is a membrane-bound structure that contains the hereditary material of the cell, the DNA.
- **Mitochondria** carry out cellular respiration and provide energy to the cells.
- **Vacuoles** store food, water, and waste for the cell.
- The **endoplasmic reticulum** is a network of tubes that transports materials for the cell.
- **Ribosomes** are structures that produce protein for the cell.
- **Golgi bodies** are structures that package and distribute protein outside the cell.

How to Create Your Left-Hand Notebook Page

Complete the following steps to create the left-hand page of your life science notebook. Use lots of color.

Step 1: Cut out the title and glue it to the top of the notebook page.
Step 2: Cut out the diagram box. Apply glue to the back and attach it below the title.
Step 3: Cut out the eight definition cards and glue each card in the correct box on the diagram.

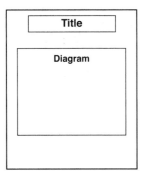

Demonstrate What You Have Learned

Observe an animal cell. Add a drop of iodine to a slide. Use the blunt end of a toothpick to gently scrape the inside lining of your cheek. Place the blunt end of the toothpick on the slide and mix it with the iodine. Place a cover slip over the solution. View the slide under a microscope. Record your observations in your life science notebook.

Animal Cell

Cell Diagram

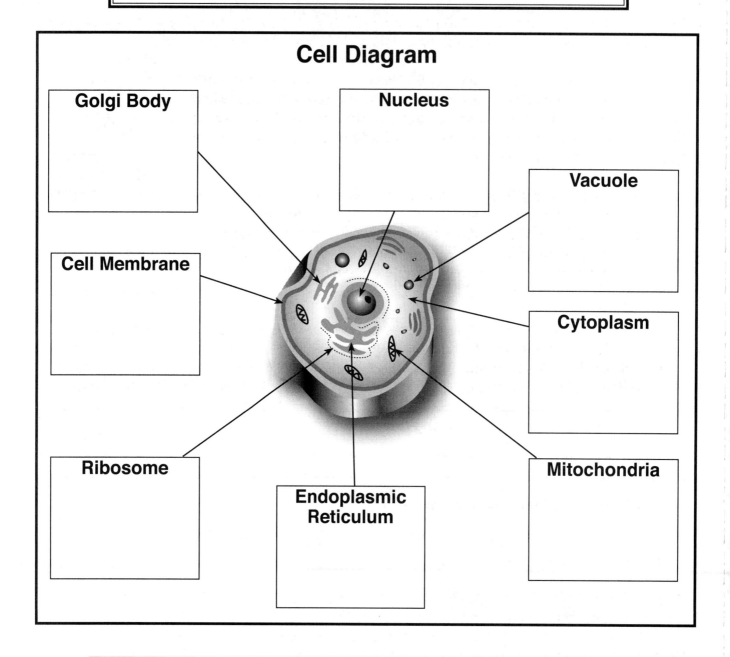

Golgi Body

Nucleus

Vacuole

Cell Membrane

Cytoplasm

Ribosome

Mitochondria

Endoplasmic Reticulum

packages and distributes protein outside the cell	control center for the cell	gel-like material that contains organelles	encloses the cell
makes protein for the cell	makes energy for the cell	transportation system for the cell	stores food, water, and waste for the cell

Mitosis

Mini-Lesson

Read the following information. Then cut out and attach this box to the right-hand page of your life science notebook. Use what you have learned to create the left-hand page.

All living things grow and repair themselves by the process of **mitosis**, cell division. This process is a series of phases or steps where two identical cells are made from one. The original cell no longer exists. Cells produced from mitosis are called **diploids** because they have two complete sets of chromosomes.

Mitosis

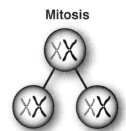

- **Phase 1 – Interphase:** DNA breaks up into short chromosomes. Each chromosome makes an exact copy of itself. Each pair is connected near the middle in a region called the **centromere**.
- **Phase 2 – Prophase:** Chromosomes are now visible; the nuclear membrane disappears, and spindle fibers called **centrioles** stretch across the cell.
- **Phase 3 – Metaphase:** Chromosomes line up along the center of the cell and attach to a spindle fiber.
- **Phase 4 – Anaphase:** Spindle fibers go to work like a tugboat, pulling each pair apart toward opposite ends of the cell.
- **Phase 5 – Telophase:** A nuclear membrane reappears around each mass of chromosomes, and the cell pinches apart in the middle. Now there are two separate cells. The nucleus of each new cell, called the **daughter cell**, has the same number and type of chromosomes as the original cell.

How to Create Your Left-Hand Notebook Page

Complete the following steps to create the left-hand page of your life science notebook. Use lots of color.

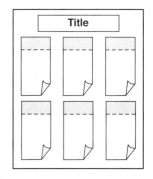

Step 1: Cut out the title and glue it to the top of the page.
Step 2: Cut out the six flap charts. Apply glue to the back of each gray tab and attach the charts below the title.
Step 3: Write the correct explanation under each flap.

Demonstrate What You Have Learned

Create a three-dimensional model that illustrates the phases in the process of mitosis. Label each phase.

Mitosis

Cell Division	Phase 1	Phase 2
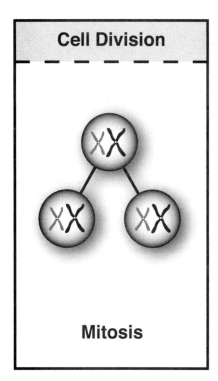	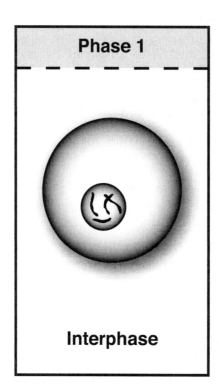	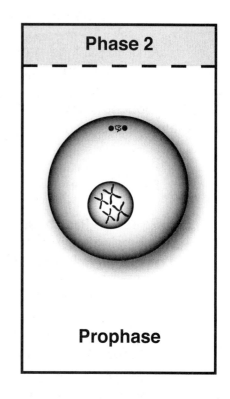
Mitosis	**Interphase**	**Prophase**

Phase 3	Phase 4	Phase 5
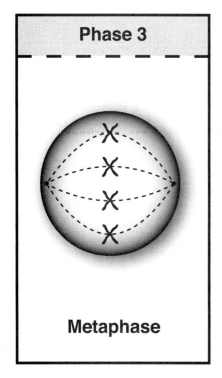	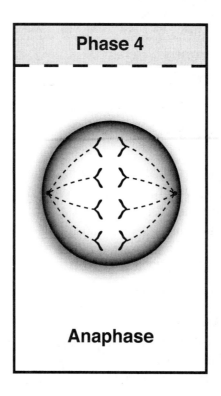	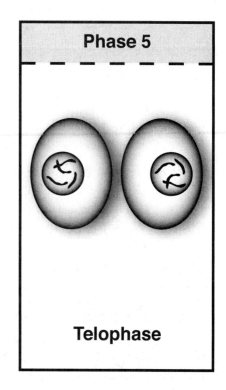
Metaphase	**Anaphase**	**Telophase**

Classification Hierarchy

Mini-Lesson

Read the following information. Then cut out and attach this box to the right-hand page of your life science notebook. Use what you have learned to create the left-hand page.

The **classification hierarchy** is a system used by scientists to organize all living things into groups based on shared characteristics. The system includes seven levels: kingdom, phylum, class, order, family, genus, and species.

Think of the classification hierarchy as an inverted pyramid. Kingdoms are at the top, and this grouping has the largest number of organisms. Each of the other six levels contains fewer types of organisms than the level before. Species is the bottom level and includes only one type of organism. As you move from the kingdom level to the species level, organisms become more closely related. There are five kingdoms in which all living things are grouped.

- The **Monera Kingdom** consists of **unicellular** (one-celled) organisms. The cell often lacks many cell parts, such as a nucleus, that are commonly found in other cells. Bacteria are a type of monera.
- The **Protist Kingdom** consists of unicellular organisms. The cell does contain a nucleus. They have moving parts and can move around within their environment. Protozoa and algae are examples of protists.
- The **Fungi Kingdom** consists of **multicellular** (many-celled) organisms. Each cell contains a nucleus. They were once thought to be plants because the cells that make up these organisms have cell walls. Fungi cannot make their own food; instead, they absorb energy from their host. Mushrooms are a type of fungi.
- The **Plant Kingdom** consists of multicellular organisms. Each cell contains a nucleus and has a cell wall. Plants make their own food using water and sunlight. All plants are part of this kingdom, including trees, grass, flowers, and algae.
- The **Animal Kingdom** consists of multicellular organisms. Each cell contains a nucleus. Animals rely on other organisms for food. Birds and lizards are animals.

How to Create Your Left-Hand Notebook Page

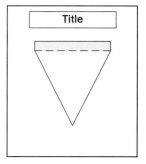

Complete the following steps to create the left-hand page of your life science notebook. Use lots of color.

Step 1: Cut out the title and glue it to the top of the page.

Step 2: Cut out the flap chart. Apply glue to the gray tab and attach the chart below the title.

Step 3: Cut out the word cards and glue on the correct level of the pyramid.

Step 3: Write a summary of the classification hierarchy system under the flap chart.

Demonstrate What You Have Learned

Create a mnemonic device to help you remember the correct order of levels in the classification hierarchy. In your life science notebook write a sentence in which the words begin with the first letters of each level of the hierarchy. For example, **K**eep **P**utting **C**ookies **O**ut **F**or **G**irl **S**couts.

Classification Hierarchy

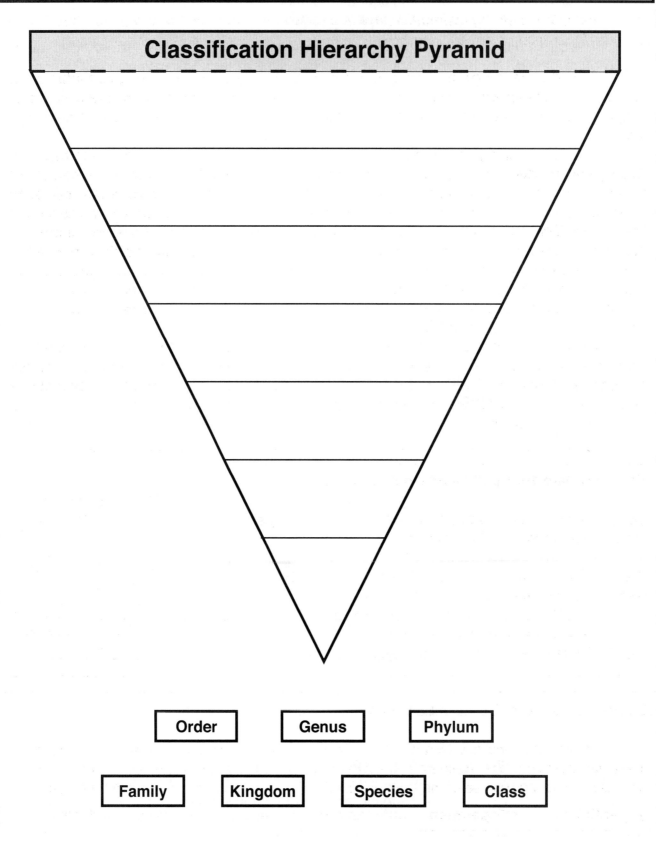

Classification Hierarchy Pyramid

Order	Genus	Phylum

Family	Kingdom	Species	Class

Monera Kingdom

Mini-Lesson

Read the following information. Then cut out and attach this box to the right-hand page of your life science notebook. Use what you have learned to create the left-hand page.

The **Monera Kingdom** contains microscopic organisms. They are **unicellular** (one-celled) organisms known as bacteria. All the organisms of this kingdom are **prokaryotic cells**; the cell has no membrane-bound nucleus and does not have specialized **organelles**, cell structures.

Scientists classify monerans into two main groups: bacteria and blue-green bacteria. **Blue-green bacteria**, also called cyanobacteria, are **producers**, organisms that can make their own food and contain chlorophyll. This moneran can be found in the slimy green stuff found on some ponds and lakes. Fish and other small animals living in or near water eat this type of bacteria for food. **Bacteria** are more common than blue-green bacteria. These monerans are **consumers** (depend on other organisms for their food). Bacteria can be classified by whether or not they need oxygen to survive. Bacteria that need oxygen are called **aerobes**. Bacteria that do not need oxygen are called **anaerobes**. Bacteria can also be classified by their shape. Round-shaped bacteria are called **cocci**, rod-shaped bacteria are called **bacilli**, and spiral-shaped bacteria are called **spirilla**.

While some bacteria are helpful, other bacteria, called **pathogens**, can be very harmful. Lyme disease, strep throat, cholera, and other diseases are pathogens that make many people ill each year. Some monerans produce **toxins** (poisons). Bacteria in spoiled food can produce toxins, causing a disease called botulism. It can affect the nervous system and even kill the person eating the spoiled food.

How to Create Your Left-Hand Notebook Page

Complete the following steps to create the left-hand page of your life science notebook. Use lots of color.

Step 1: Cut out the title and glue it to the top of the notebook page.
Step 2: Cut out the flap chart. Cut on the solid lines to create eight vocabulary flaps. Apply glue to the back of the gray tab and attach the chart below the title.
Step 3: Write the correct definition under each flap.

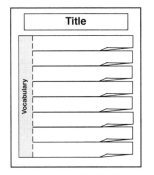

Demonstrate What You Have Learned

Harmful bacteria are all around us. There are many methods to control the growth of these harmful monerans. Research one of the topics listed below. Use the information to create a poster promoting the use of the method to fight disease and sickness caused by bacteria.

antibiotics   refrigeration   disinfectant   antiseptic   vaccines   antibodies

Monera Kingdom

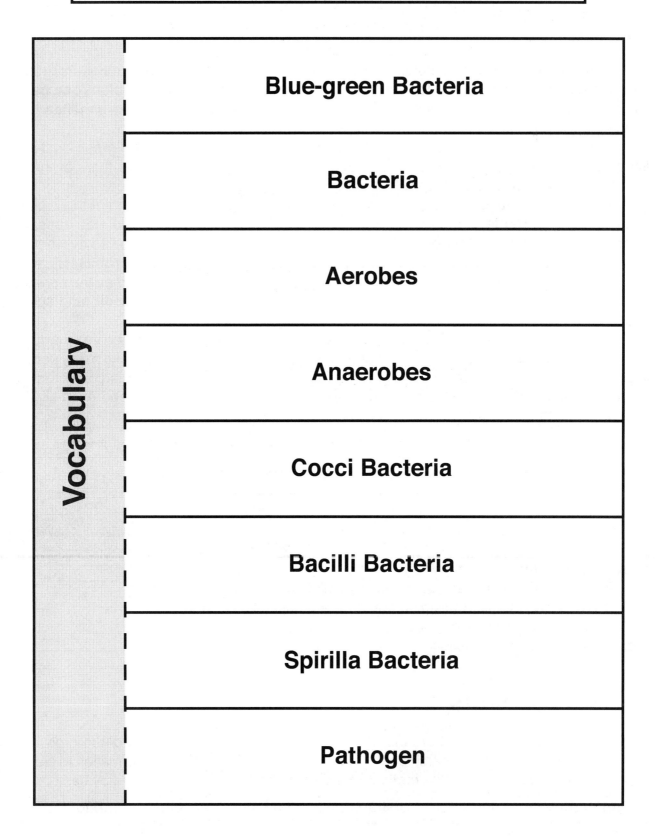

Vocabulary

Blue-green Bacteria

Bacteria

Aerobes

Anaerobes

Cocci Bacteria

Bacilli Bacteria

Spirilla Bacteria

Pathogen

Protist Kingdom

Mini-Lesson

Read the following information. Then cut out and attach this box to the right-hand page of your life science notebook. Use what you have learned to create the left-hand page.

The **Protist Kingdom** consists of microscopic organisms that are **unicellular** (one-celled). The cell contains a nucleus. They have moving parts and can move about within their environment. They thrive in moist environments such as rotting logs, damp soil, or the bodies of other organisms. However, most live in a body of water such as a pond, river, swamp, or an ocean.

Protist Classification

- **Plant-like protists** are also known as **algae**. Algae contain chlorophyll and make their own food through photosynthesis. There are four major pigments found in algae: red, yellow-brown, green, and blue-green. Other types of plant-like protists are diatoms, dinoflagellates, and euglenoids. They produce oxygen that many living things need to survive.
- **Animal-like protists** are called **protozoans**. They need to get food from their environment since they cannot make it themselves. Protozoans move in one of three ways to get that food. **Cilia** are multiple small, hair-like structures lining the cell membrane that move the cell along as if they were oars on a boat. A paramecium is an example. **Flagella** are whip-like structures that push the cell along. A trypanosoma, which causes African sleeping sickness, is an example. **Pseudopods**, or false feet, extend forward, then pull the rest of the body along. Pseudopods are used to reach out and capture food. An amoeba is an example.
- **Fungus-like protists** contain a substance called chitin in their cell wall and reproduce by forming spores. They usually do not move. Slime molds and water molds are examples.

How to Create Your Left-Hand Notebook Page

Complete the following steps to create the left-hand page of your life science notebook. Use lots of color.

Step 1: Cut out the title and glue it to the top of the notebook page.
Step 2: Cut out the three flap charts. Apply glue to the back of each gray tab and attach the charts below the title.
Step 3: Write the correct description under each flap.

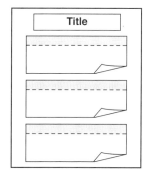

Demonstrate What You Have Learned

Use a microscope to view samples of pond or river water. Draw and identify any organisms you observe in your life science notebook. Use your science textbook or online sources if you need help.

Protist Kingdom

Animal-like Protist

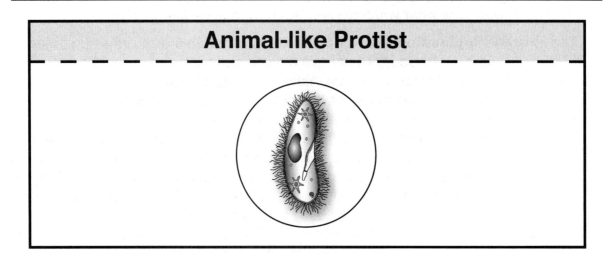

Plant-like Protist

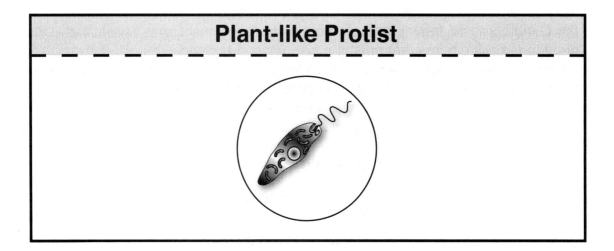

Fungus-like Protist

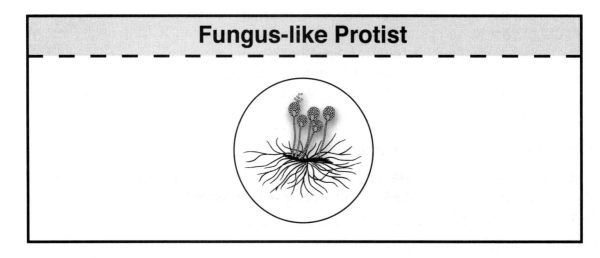

Fungi Kingdom

Mini-Lesson

Read the following information. Then cut out and attach this box to the right-hand page of your life science notebook. Use what you have learned to create the left-hand page.

The **Fungi Kingdom** consists of organisms that are **multicellular**, made up of several or many cells. All fungi are made up of **eukaryotic cells**, which means they contain a membrane-bound nucleus. Fungi are made up of long individual strands called **hyphae**. The hyphae produce enzymes that break down food into substances the fungi can easily absorb.

Fungi were once thought to be plants because the cells that make up these organisms have cell walls. Fungi are different from plants in two ways. The cell walls of fungi are made up of a material called **chitin** rather than cellulose, and the cells cannot make their own food because they lack **chlorophyll**, the chemical needed to carry out **photosynthesis**. Since fungi cannot make their own food, they are classified as a **heterotroph**. Fungi get their energy by feeding on living or dead organisms; this causes the organism to rot.

Fungi play a vital role in the decomposition of organic matter. Breaking down organic matter releases nitrogen, carbon, and oxygen into the soil and atmosphere. Some fungi are used to make antibiotics like penicillin to kill bacteria that cause infections in humans.

Common Fungi

- Mushrooms are the fruiting body or reproductive part of a fungus. Some mushrooms are good to eat while others are poisonous.
- Mold is formed by hyphae and looks woolly or furry as the hyphae grow up and release more mold spores from their tips. It is found on rotting foods, such as bread and fruit.
- Yeast are a single-celled fungi that makes bread rise.

How to Create Your Left-Hand Notebook Page

Complete the following steps to create the left-hand page of your life science notebook. Use lots of color.

Step 1: Cut out the title and glue it to the top of the page.

Step 2: Cut out the graphic organizer chart. Apply glue to the back and attach the chart below the title.

Step 3: Cut out the word cards and glue one on each arrow. Write the correct description in the boxes below each arrow.

Step 4: Cut out the three flap charts. Apply glue to the back of each gray tab and glue the charts at the bottom of the page. Write the correct definition under each flap.

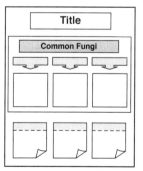

Demonstrate What You Have Learned

Create a T-chart in your life science notebook. List the benefits of fungi and the harmful effects of fungi. Use your science textbook or online sources to help you.

Fungi Kingdom

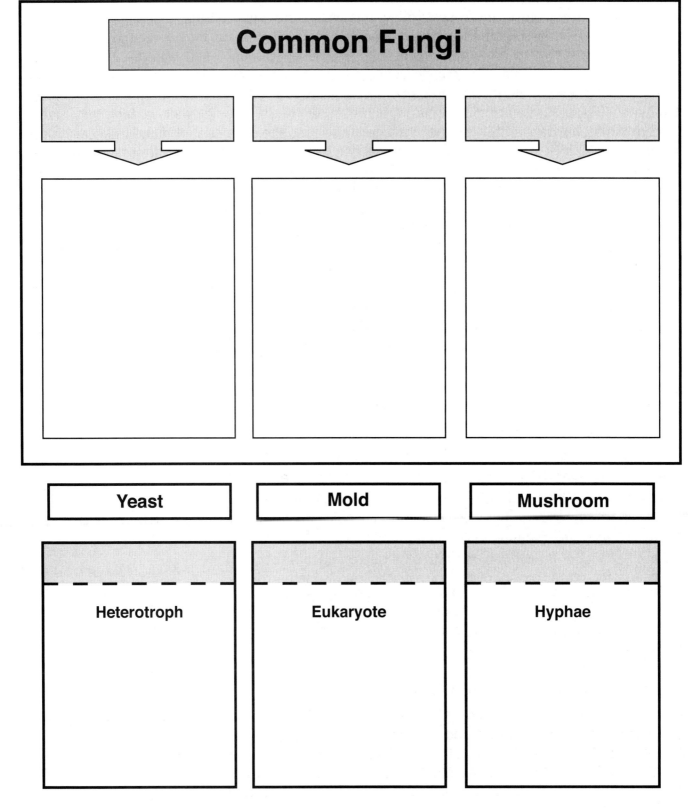

Common Fungi

Yeast	Mold	Mushroom
Heterotroph	Eukaryote	Hyphae

Plant Kingdom

Mini-Lesson

Read the following information. Then cut out and attach this box to the right-hand page of your life science notebook. Use what you have learned to create the left-hand page.

The **Plant Kingdom** consists of organisms that are **multicellular**, made up of several or many cells. The cells are surrounded with a cell wall. Cells contain membrane-bound organelles that allow them to carry on life processes as plants. Plants make their own food in a process called **photosynthesis**. Because plants can make their own food, scientists classify them as **producers**. The Plant Kingdom can be divided into two major groups: vascular plants and nonvascular plants.

Vascular plants have tube-like structures inside the plant to carry food, water, and minerals to all parts of the plant. Vascular plants do not need direct contact with water. As a result, they are able to grow in almost every kind of environment. Vascular plants produce leaves, stems, and roots. The leaves make food for the plant with the help of sunlight and chlorophyll. Xylem and phloem are tube-like structures that make up the transportation system of vascular plants. The **xylem** tubes transport water from the roots to the leaves. The **phloem** tubes are responsible for moving food down from the leaves to other parts of the plant. Vascular plants include trees and ferns.

Nonvascular plants do not have tube-like structures to carry food and water through the plant. Nonvascular plants do not have leaves, stems, or roots. Instead, nonvascular plants have hair-like **rhizoids** to anchor them to the ground and to absorb water and minerals. Most nonvascular plants are found in moist areas. They include mosses, hornworts, and liverworts.

How to Create Your Left-Hand Notebook Page

Complete the following steps to create the left-hand page of your life science notebook. Use lots of color.

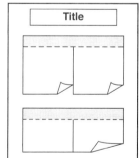

Step 1: Cut out the title and glue it to the top of the page.

Step 2: Cut out the flap chart. Apply glue to the back of the gray tab and attach the chart below the title. Write the correct definition for each type of plant under each flap. Cut out the two picture cards and glue each card in the correct box on the chart.

Step 3: Cut out the second flap chart. Apply glue to the back of the gray tab and attach the chart at the bottom of the page. Cut out the two definition cards and glue each card in the correct box on the chart.

Demonstrate What You Have Learned

Explore the role of stems in the transportation of water in plants. Fill a glass beaker half full of water. Add several drops of red food coloring to the water. Cut one inch off the end of a celery stalk and discard the end. Place the stalk into the beaker. View the celery stalk after 24 hours. Is celery a vascular or nonvascular plant? Explain. Record the answer in your life science notebook.

Plant Kingdom

Two Types of Plants

Vascular Plants	Nonvascular Plants

moss on a rock

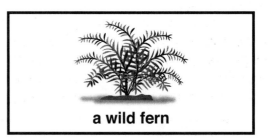

a wild fern

Transport System of Vascular Plants

Xylem Tubes	Phloem Tubes

transports food down from
the leaves to other parts
of the plant

transports water from
the roots to the leaves

Vascular Plants

Mini-Lesson

Read the following information. Then cut out and attach this box to the right-hand page of your life science notebook. Use what you have learned to create the left-hand page.

Vascular plants have tube-like structures that move food and water from one part of the plant to another. This group of plants can be divided into three groups: filicineae, gymnosperms, and angiosperms.

Filicineae, or ferns, reproduce by spores. If you look on the bottom of fern leaves, or fronds, you may see small, dot-like structures. They are the spore cases. When the spore cases burst open, tiny spores are released. They will become new ferns. Ferns grow in many different places; however, they prefer soil and air that are moist. There are a great number of ferns that grow in the tropics. They are also commonly found in damp forest areas.

Gymnosperms are called "naked seed" plants because their seeds are not formed inside a fruit. Many gymnosperm plants are called **conifers** because they produce their seeds inside of cones. Their leaves may look like needles. They are often known as **evergreen** plants because they do not lose all of their leaves at one time. Redwood trees, the tallest and oldest trees known in the world, are gymnosperms.

Angiosperms, or flowering plants, reproduce by making seeds inside of fruits. People eat the fruits of many of the angiosperms, such as bananas and tomatoes. Some of the flowers and fruit we do not even notice. Most **deciduous** trees, such as maples, oaks, and elms, flower in the spring and lose all of their leaves in the fall of the year. The flowers may be the same color as the leaves, so we do not always notice them.

How to Create Your Left-Hand Notebook Page

Complete the following steps to create the left-hand page of your life science notebook. Use lots of color.

Step 1: Cut out the title and glue it to the top of the notebook page.
Step 2: Cut out the three pockets. Fold back the gray tabs on the dotted lines. Apply glue to the tabs and attach the pockets below the title.
Step 3: Cut out the word strips. Pace each strip in the correct pocket.

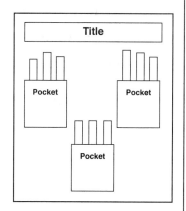

Demonstrate What You Have Learned

Ferns reproduce from spores, not flowers. Look on the underside of a fertile frond at the clusters of brown dots. The dots are made up of many spore cases. Use a toothpick to open a spore case. Examine the spores with a magnifying glass. Record your observations in your life science notebook.

Vascular Plants

Filicinaea Plants

Gymnosperm Plants

Angiosperm Plants

ferns
leaves called fronds
conifer trees
tulips
reproduce from spores
naked seeds
redwood trees
seeds inside fruit
deciduous trees

Photosynthesis, Respiration, and Transpiration

Mini-Lesson

Read the following information. Then cut out and attach this box to the right-hand page of your life science notebook. Use what you have learned to create the left-hand page.

Photosynthesis, respiration, and transpiration are related processes that take place in the leaves of green plants.

Photosynthesis is the process green plants use to produce energy or glucose. **Glucose** (sugar) is the food plants need to live. Leaves take in carbon dioxide from the air through the **stomata**, tiny openings. Water and minerals from the soil travel through the roots and stems of the plant to cells in the leaves. Here, they chemically combine with **chlorophyll**, a green pigment present in all green plants. Chlorophyll is stored inside plant cells in organelles called **chloroplasts**. It is responsible for the absorption of light used to produce glucose. Glucose is the usable food for green plants. During this process, the leaf releases oxygen back into the environment as a waste product through the stomata. Photosynthesis is a chemical reaction that can be shown as a word equation.

$$\text{Carbon Dioxide} + \text{Water} + \text{Light} \longrightarrow \text{Glucose} + \text{Oxygen}$$

Respiration is a continuous cycle of the exchange of gases and water between plants and the environment. Respiration is important to the process of plants making food. The stomata, in the leaves of the plant, take in carbon dioxide to produce glucose and give off oxygen as waste during photosynthesis.

Transpiration is the process whereby plants absorb water through the roots and then give off water vapor through the stomata in the leaves. Transpiration is important to the process of plants making food. The process provides the plant with the water needed to produce glucose during photosynthesis.

How to Create Your Left-Hand Notebook Page

Complete the following steps to create the left-hand page of your life science notebook. Use lots of color.

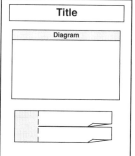

Step 1: Cut out the title and glue it to the top of the notebook page.

Step 2: Cut out the diagram chart. Apply glue to the back of the gray tab and attach it below the title. Cut out the word cards and glue each card in the correct box on the chart.

Step 3: Cut out the flap chart. Cut on the solid line to create two vocabulary flaps. Apply glue to the back of the gray tab and attach the chart at the bottom of the page. Write the correct definition under each flap.

Demonstrate What You Have Learned

Place a wood block on a section of lawn. Remove the block after seven days. Record your observations and write an explanation of the condition of the grass in your life science notebook.

Photosynthesis, Respiration, and Transpiration

Photosynthesis Diagram

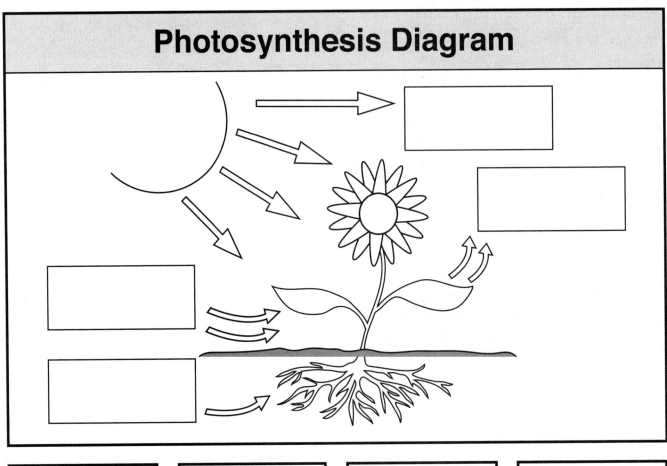

Water	Carbon Dioxide	Light	Oxygen

	Respiration
	Transpiration

Flowering Plants

Angiosperms are flowering plants. Flowers perform the job of reproduction for the plant. Most flowers have four parts to them: sepal, petals, the stamens, and the pistil.

- The **sepal** is green and looks like leaves. The sepal has two functions: to protect the flower bud until it opens and support the flower after it blooms.
- The flower **petals** are often brightly colored or unusually shaped to attract pollinators, such as butterflies and bees.
- The **stamen** is the male reproductive part of a flower. Each stamen actually consists of two parts put together. The **anther** is an enlarged part of the stamen. It grows on a thin, stalk-like part that is called the **filament**. The anther produces **pollen** or sperm cells for reproduction. The sperm cells are very important in the reproduction of a flowering plant.
- The **pistil** is the female reproductive part of the flower. A pistil has three important parts. At the top of the pistil is a flattened part that is called the **stigma**. The stigma is attached to a tube, which is called the **style**. At the base of the style is the **ovary**. It contains the **ovules** or egg cells for reproduction.

Pollination is the transfer of pollen to a stigma of a flowering plant to allow fertilization. After pollination, the flower becomes fruit. The fruit provides a covering for the seeds. Some flowers are **self-pollinators**, having everything they need to pollinate in just one plant. Other flowers are **cross-pollinators** and need another plant to make the pollination complete.

How to Create Your Left-Hand Notebook Page

Complete the following steps to create the left-hand page of your life science notebook. Use lots of color.

Step 1: Cut out the title and glue it to the top of the notebook page.

Step 2: Cut out the diagram chart. Apply glue to the back and attach it below the title.

Step 3: Cut out the four definition cards and glue each card in the correct box on the chart.

Demonstrate What You Have Learned

Cut open a flower. Locate and identify each of its parts. Draw a chart similar to the one at the right in your life science notebook. Carefully, separate each part from the flower and tape it in the correct box on the chart.

petal	anther	filament
sepal	eggs	pistil

Flowering Plants

Flower Diagram

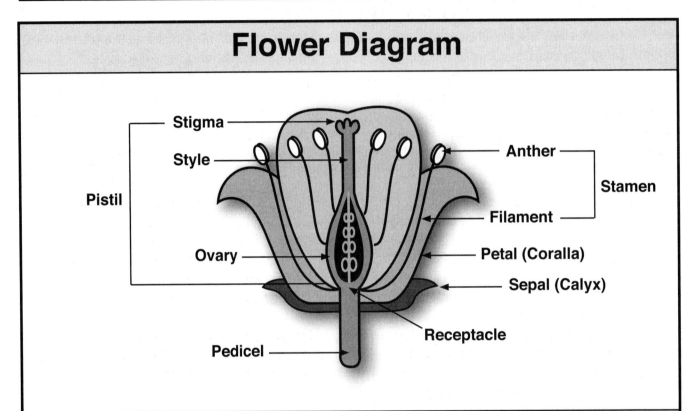

Pistil	Stamen	Petal	Sepal

protects the flower bud until it opens and supports the flower after it blooms	attracts pollinators	the female reproductive part of the flower	the male reproductive part of the flower

Seeds

Mini-Lesson

Read the following information. Then cut out and attach this box to the right-hand page of your life science notebook. Use what you have learned to create the left-hand page.

Seeds form in the fruit of **angiosperms**, or flowering plants. Seeds have three main parts: seed coat, embryo, and cotyledon. The **seed coat** protects the new plant forming inside the seed. The **embryo** contains all the parts needed to become a new plant. The **cotyledon** is the tiny seed leaves that absorb food and allow the plant to begin its growth. The process of a plant growing from a seed is called **germination**.

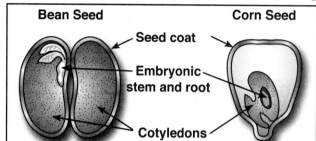

Dicot and Monocot Plants

- The prefix *di-* means "two." **Dicots** get their name from having seeds with two cotyledons. The flower parts of a dicot plant come in multiples of four or five. The veins form a netted pattern all over the leaf. Leaves come in many different shapes and sizes. The stems are normally woody. The **phloem** and **xylem**, tubes that carry nutrients and water up and down the stem, are arranged in a ring. Dicot plants have a taproot system.

- The prefix *mono-* means "one." **Monocots** get their name from having seeds with one cotyledon. The flower parts on a monocot plant come in multiples of three. The leaves are long and narrow, with their veins arranged in parallel lines. In the stem, the phloem and xylem tubes are in bundles scattered throughout the stem. Monocot plants have fibrous roots.

How to Create Your Left-Hand Notebook Page

Complete the following steps to create the left-hand page of your life science notebook. Use lots of color.

Step 1: Cut out the title and glue it to the top of the page.

Step 2: Cut out the diagram chart. Apply glue to the back and attach it below the title. Label the parts of each seed diagram.

Step 3: Cut out the second chart. Apply glue to the back and attach it at the bottom of the page. Fill in the chart with the correct information.

Demonstrate What You Have Learned

Soak several lima beans in water for 24 hours. Peel the seed coat off the seed. Gently pry the seed apart using your thumbnail or a toothpick. Examine the seed using a magnifying glass. Is a lima bean a dicot or monocot seed? Explain. Write your answer in your life science notebook.

Seeds

Seed Diagrams

Dicot Seed

Monocot Seed

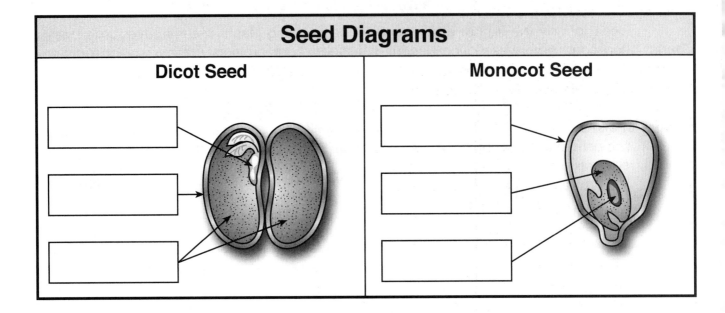

Dicot and Monocot Plants

Characteristic	Dicot	Monocot
seeds		
flowers		
leaves		
stems		
roots		

Trees

Mini-Lesson

Read the following information. Then cut out and attach this box to the right-hand page of your life science notebook. Use what you have learned to create the left-hand page.

Trees are plants with woody stems. There are two types of trees: deciduous and evergreen. **Deciduous** trees lose all of their leaves for part of the year. **Evergreen** trees don't lose all of their leaves at the same time; they always have some green foliage.

Parts of a Tree

- The **crown** consists of the leaves and branches at the top of a tree. The crown shades the roots, collects energy from the sun, and releases water to keep the tree cool.
- The **leaves** are the food factories of a tree. They convert energy into food, or glucose.
- The **roots** absorb water and nutrients from the soil, store sugar, and anchor the tree in the ground
- The **trunk**, or stem, supports the crown and gives the tree its shape and strength. The trunk consists of several layers of tissue. The **bark** is made up of dead cells. It protects the tree from such things as insects and disease. The thin layer of living cells just inside the bark is called the **cambium**. It is the part of the tree that makes new cells, allowing the tree to grow wider each year. The **xylem** tissue transports water from the roots to the leaves. The **phloem** tissue is responsible for moving food down from the leaves to other parts of the plant. The xylem and phloem tissues form rings around the **heartwood**, the center of the tree. It is made up of dead cells. The main function of the heartwood is to support the tree. The **pith** is the tiny dark spot of spongy living cells in the center of the heartwood. Essential nutrients are carried up through the pith to all parts of the tree.

How to Create Your Left-Hand Notebook Page

Complete the following steps to create the left-hand page of your life science notebook. Use lots of color.

Step 1: Cut out the title and glue it to the top of the notebook page.
Step 2: Cut out the diagram chart. Apply glue to the back and attach it below the title.
Step 3: Write the function of each part of a tree trunk in the correct box on the chart below the diagram.

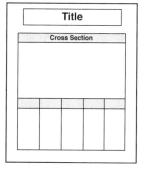

Demonstrate What You Have Learned

Examine a cross section of a tree trunk. You may need to find a picture online. Draw and label a diagram of the section in your life science notebook.

Trees

Cross Section of a Tree Trunk

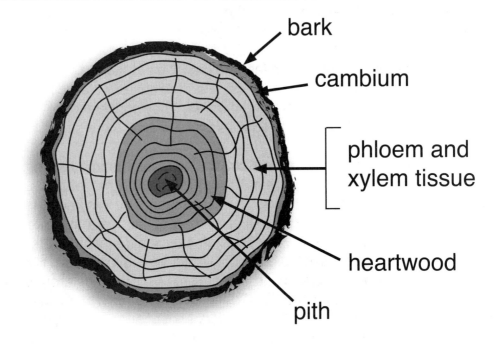

bark

cambium

phloem and xylem tissue

heartwood

pith

Bark	Cambium	Phloem and Xylem	Heartwood	Pith
Function:	Function:	Function:	Function:	Function:

Animal Kingdom Part 1

Mini-Lesson

Read the following information. Then cut out and attach this box to the right-hand page of your life science notebook. Use what you have learned to create the left-hand page.

When identifying animals, scientists look to see if the animal has a backbone. If the animal does not have a backbone, it is called an **invertebrate**. Invertebrates make up 95 percent of all the known animals.

Common Invertebrates

- **Sponges** are animals. Their bodies are made up of many holes or pores that are used for feeding. Sponges are tube-shaped with an opening at the top.
- **Hollow-bodies** are animals that have hollow bodies with one opening. The body openings are surrounded by tentacles. Some hollow-bodied animals have stinging cells on their tentacles. For example, jellyfish, coral, and sea anemones.
- **Worms** are divided into three groups. There are worms with flattened bodies such as planarians, tapeworms, and flukes; worms with round, tube-like bodies such as pinworms; and worms with segmented bodies such as earthworms and leeches.
- **Mollusks** are soft-bodied animals, usually with a shell, such as snails, clams, and oysters.
- **Arthropods** are animals with segmented bodies, jointed legs, and a hard outer skeleton. For example, insects, spiders, and lobsters are arthropods.
- **Echinoderms** are animals with skin that usually has warty projections or spines. This group includes animals such as starfish and sea urchins.

How to Create Your Left-Hand Notebook Page

Complete the following steps to create the left-hand page of your life science notebook. Use lots of color.

Step 1: Cut out the title and glue it to the top of the page.
Step 2: Cut out the flap chart. Cut on the solid lines to create six flaps. Apply glue to the back of the gray center section of the chart and attach it below the title.
Step 3: Cut out the examples of invertebrates and glue them on the correct flap.
Step 4: Write the correct description under each flap.

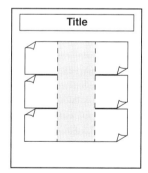

Demonstrate What You Have Learned

Research one of the invertebrates listed in the lesson. Create a fact cube to display your research. On one face of the cube write the animal's name. On the other faces write an interesting fact you learned.

Animal Kingdom Part 1

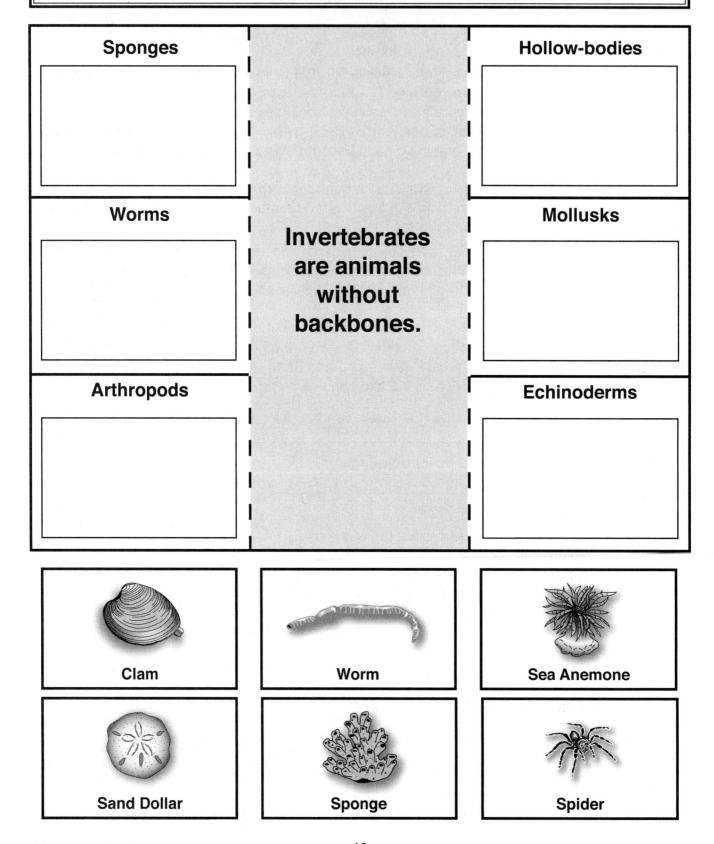

Sponges

Worms

Arthropods

Invertebrates are animals without backbones.

Hollow-bodies

Mollusks

Echinoderms

Clam

Worm

Sea Anemone

Sand Dollar

Sponge

Spider

Animal Kingdom Part 2

Mini-Lesson

Read the following information. Then cut out and attach this box to the right-hand page of your life science notebook. Use what you have learned to create the left-hand page.

When identifying animals, scientists look to see if the animal has a backbone. If the animal has a backbone, it is called a **vertebrate**. They are the most complex and familiar animals. You are a vertebrate. If you run your hand down your back, you can feel your backbone. Your backbone is made of many small bones and cartilage called **vertebrae**. Vertebrates include fish, amphibians, reptiles, birds, and mammals. Each group has specific characteristics.

- **Fish** live in water, breathe using special organs called gills, and lay eggs. They are cold-blooded (body temperature changes with the temperature of their surroundings). Some examples are sharks, trout, and salmon.
- **Amphibians** are cold-blooded and lay eggs in water or moist ground. Most young have gills, and most adults have lungs. For example, frogs and newts are amphibians.
- **Reptiles** are cold-blooded and are covered with dry scaly skin. They usually lay soft-shelled eggs. Several examples are snakes, lizards, and alligators.
- **Birds** are warm-blooded (have a constant body temperature). They have feathers, toothless beaked jaws, and lay hard-shelled eggs. Examples of birds are eagles, flamingos, and doves.
- **Mammals** are warm-blooded, have hair at some point in their lives, and feed their young with milk. Some examples include humans, whales, zebras, and lions.

How to Create Your Left-Hand Notebook Page

Complete the following steps to create the left-hand page of your life science notebook. Use lots of color.

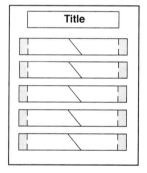

Step 1: Cut out the title and glue it to the top of the notebook page.

Step 2: Cut out the puzzle pieces. Match each vocabulary word with the correct picture. Apply glue to the back of each gray tab, and attach the matching pieces below the title.

Step 3: List the correct animal characteristics under the flap of each matched pair.

Demonstrate What You Have Learned

Go online and watch the video Vertebrates at <https://www.youtube.com/watch?v=IT_y1jOoaXc>. Write 10 interesting facts you learned about vertebrates in your life science notebook.

Animal Kingdom Part 2

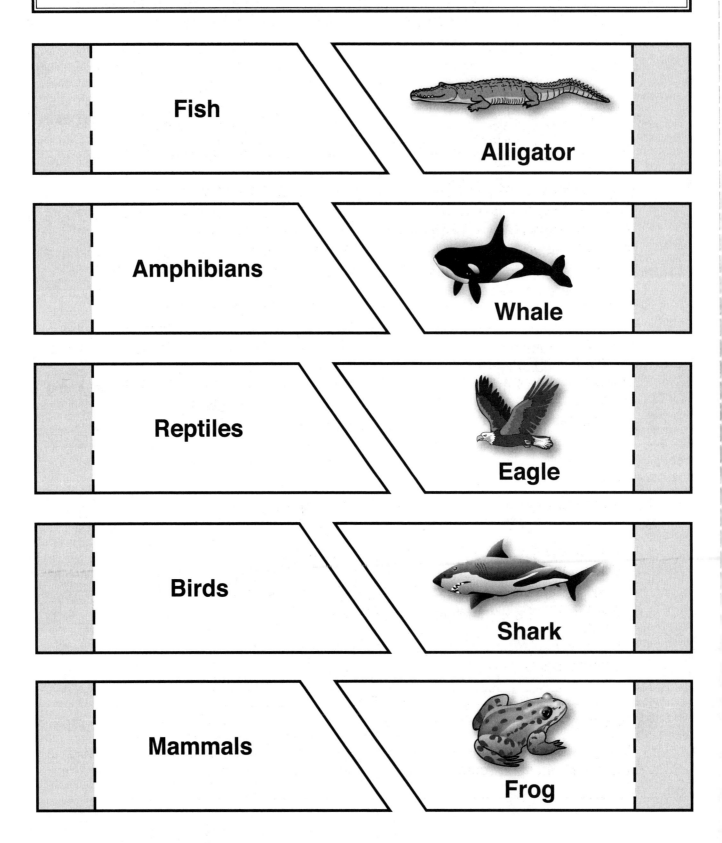

Fish

Alligator

Amphibians

Whale

Reptiles

Eagle

Birds

Shark

Mammals

Frog

Genetics

Mini-Lesson

Read the following information. Then cut out and attach this box to the right-hand page of your life science notebook. Use what you have learned to create the left-hand page.

Scientists studied cells for many years before they discovered how **traits** (characteristics) of the parents, such as eye and hair color, were passed on to their offspring. By the end of the nineteenth century, scientists had learned the secret code of **heredity** (passing physical and character traits from one generation to another). They found that traits are controlled by genes made up of DNA located on the chromosomes found in the nucleus of plant and animal cells.

- Inside every **cell** is a genetic code or chemical blueprint for how the organism looks and functions.
- The **nucleus** is the most important structure inside a cell. It can be thought of as the control center of the cell.
- **Chromosomes** are tiny rod-shaped strands of genetic material found inside the nucleus of a cell. Humans have 23 pairs of chromosomes in each cell. One set of chromosomes for each pair comes from a person's mother, and the other set of chromosomes comes from the father.
- Chromosomes are made from molecules of **DNA** (deoxyribonucleic acid). The DNA molecule is a long, coiled double helix that resembles a twisted ladder. The rungs of the ladder are made of molecules called bases. The sides of the ladder are made up of phosphate and sugar molecules.
- A **gene** is a short section of the DNA ladder. The order of the molecules on the ladder in that section form a **genetic code**, instructions for creating specific proteins for the development of a trait passed from parent to offspring.

How to Create Your Left-Hand Notebook Page

Complete the following steps to create the left-hand page of your life science notebook. Use lots of color.

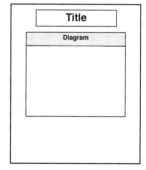

Step 1: Cut out the title and glue it to the top of the page.

Step 2: Cut out the diagram box. Apply glue to the back of the gray tab and attach the chart below the title. Cut out the word cards and glue each card in the correct box on the chart.

Step 3: Write an explanation of the relationships among the cell, chromosomes, DNA, and genes under the flap.

Demonstrate What You Have Learned

Design a three-dimensional model that illustrates the basic DNA structure. Use your science textbook or online sources if you need help.

Genetics

Diagram

Relationships Among the Cell, Chromosomes, DNA, and Genes

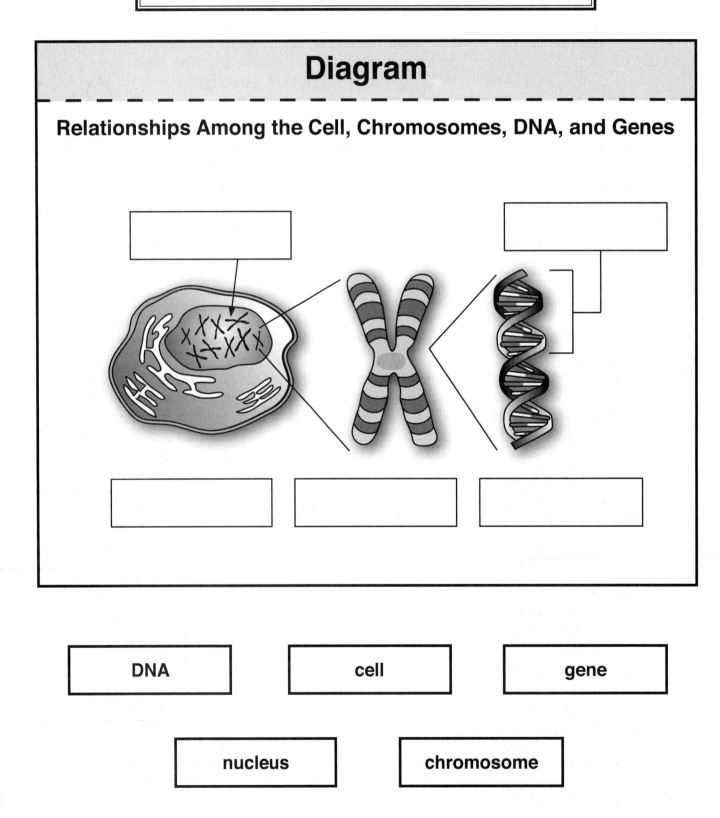

DNA

cell

gene

nucleus

chromosome

Heredity

Mini-Lesson

Read the following information. Then cut out and attach this box to the right-hand page of your science notebook. Use what you have learned to create the left-hand page.

The **characteristics** of all living things are called traits. Every living thing is a collection of **inherited traits**, characteristics passed down to an individual by the parents. These traits are controlled by genes made up of DNA and located on chromosomes found in the nucleus of cells. Traits are passed on to new cells during meiosis.

Gregor Mendel was the first person to describe how traits are inherited. His studies of the inherited traits of pea plants led to the **Laws of Dominance**, principles of genetics. He noticed that genes always came in pairs. Every organism that reproduces sexually receives two genes for every trait. A trait may be **dominant** (stronger), and that trait will show up in the organism if only one of the genes has that trait. If a trait is **recessive** (weaker), it will not show up in the organism unless the organism inherits two recessive genes.

Scientists use a **Punnett square**, designed by Reginald Punnett, to predict all possible gene combinations for the offspring of two parents. The square consists of four boxes. The square is filled in by writing one gene for each parent in each box. Each box represents possible gene combinations.

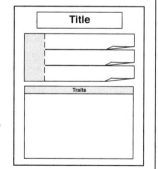

The Punnett square to the right shows the cross between two tall pea plants. Each one has one tall gene and one short gene.

T = Tall gene (dominant trait) and **t** = short gene (recessive trait). The genetic makeup of an organism is its genotype. The **genotype** (genetic makeup) of the mother is Tt, and the genotype of the father is Tt. They each have a tall gene and a short gene, but because the tall gene is dominant, both plants appear tall. There are three possible genotypes for the offspring: **TT**, **Tt**, and **tt**. Using the Punnett square, scientists can predict that 75 percent of the offspring will be tall plants. Only a plant that inherits two short genes (tt) will be short.

How to Create Your Left-Hand Notebook Page

Complete the following steps to create the left-hand page of your life science notebook. Use lots of color.

Step 1: Cut out the title and glue it to the top of the page.

Step 2: Cut out the flap chart. Cut on the solid lines to create three flaps. Apply glue to the back of the gray tab and attach the chart below the title. Write the correct definition under each flap.

Step 3: Cut out the second chart. Apply glue to the back and attach it at the bottom of the page. Complete the chart.

Demonstrate What You Have Learned

Draw a Punnett square in your life science notebook. Complete the square for eye color. The mother has the dominant gene for brown eyes, and her genotype is **BB**. The father has the recessive gene for blue eyes. His genotype is **bb**.

Heredity

Inherited Traits

Laws of Dominance

Punnett Square

Common Mendelian Traits
Do you have any of these traits? Which parent also has these traits?

D = Dominant Trait; r = Recessive Trait	You	Mother	Father
Tongue Folding (r): ability to fold the tip of your tongue back upon the main body of the tongue without using your teeth	Yes/No	Yes/No	Yes/No
Detached Earlobes (D): earlobes not directly attached to your head; free-hanging	Yes/No	Yes/No	Yes/No
Attached Earlobes (r): earlobes directly attached to the head	Yes/No	Yes/No	Yes/No
Dimples (D): natural smile produces dimples in one or both cheeks or a dimple in the center of the chin	Yes/No	Yes/No	Yes/No
Widow's Peak (D): hairline comes to a point in the middle of forehead	Yes/No	Yes/No	Yes/No
Bent little finger (D): little finger curves in toward other fingers	Yes/No	Yes/No	Yes/No
Freckles (D): circular pattern of skin coloration	Yes/No	Yes/No	Yes/No
Clockwise Whorl (D): hair on the crown of your head turns clockwise	Yes/No	Yes/No	Yes/No
Counterclockwise Whorl (r): hair on the crown of your head turns counterclockwise	Yes/No	Yes/No	Yes/No
Second Toe Longest (D): second toe is longer than the big toe	Yes/No	Yes/No	Yes/No

Meiosis

Mini-Lesson

Read the following information. Then cut out and attach this box to the right-hand page of your life science notebook. Use what you have learned to create the left-hand page.

Meiosis is the process of cell division that produces sperm and egg cells for sexual reproduction. This process occurs in plants, animals, and some fungi. When meiosis is complete, four cells are made from one. The new cells are called **haploids** and only have half the DNA of the original cell. The process occurs in two steps: Meiosis I and Meiosis II.

Meiosis

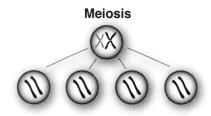

- **Meiosis I**: The cell copies its **DNA**, genetic material, which is found in the cell's nucleus in rod-shaped structures called **chromosomes**. The nucleus divides first, and then the cytoplasm divides. The nucleus disappears. The pairs of chromosomes line up in the center of the cell. Then the members of each pair separate and move to opposite ends of the cell. Next, the cell pinches in between the two sets of chromosomes. A nucleus forms around each set of chromosomes, forming two identical cells. Each new cell, called a **daughter cell**, has an exact copy of the chromosomes that were in the parent cell.

- **Meiosis II**: Each newly formed daughter cell divides once again. However, the chromosomes do not replicate themselves before dividing. In this way, one original parent cell produces four reproductive cells called haploids. Each haploid contains one-half the number of chromosomes as the original parent cell and, therefore, only half the amount of genetic material.

How to Create Your Left-Hand Notebook Page

Complete the following steps to create the left-hand page of your life science notebook. Use lots of color.

Step 1: Cut out the title and glue it to the top of the page.
Step 2: Cut out the flap chart. Apply glue to the back of the gray center section and attach the chart below the title.
Step 3: Write the correct explanation under each flap.

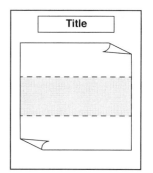

Demonstrate What You Have Learned

Create a three-dimensional model that illustrates the phases in the process of meiosis.

Meiosis

Meiosis I: First Cell Division

Parent cell   **Cell divides**

Two daughter
cells are formed.

**Meiosis is the process of cell division that produces
sperm and egg cells for sexual reproduction.**

Meiosis II: Second Cell Division

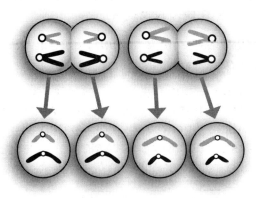

The two daughter
cells divide.

Four sex cells
are formed.

Biomes

Mini-Lesson

Read the following information. Then cut out and attach this box to the right-hand page of your life science notebook. Use what you have learned to create the left-hand page.

Biomes are regions of the world with similar climate (weather and temperature), animals, and plants. There are five major biomes.

The **aquatic biome** consists of any part of Earth that is covered with water. This includes freshwater and salt water. The aquatic biome can be further divided into freshwater, marine, wetland, coral reef, and estuaries. These subdivisions are based on the salt content of the water, the aquatic plants that live there, and the aquatic animals that thrive there.

The **desert biome** has very little vegetation. Common plants are cacti and sagebrush. Lizards and rattlesnakes have adapted to the extreme temperature. The deserts of Africa are extremely hot during the winters and warm throughout the rest of the year. There are also cold deserts, such as those in Antarctica. These deserts are extremely cold during the winter and cold during the other seasons.

The **forest biome** is the largest. The major plants are trees. It has a wide variety of animals, insects, and microscopic organisms. The forest biome can be divided based on the region's climate and types of trees. The forest biomes are rain forest, temperate, chaparral, alpine, and taiga.

The **grassland biome** is made up of rolling hills covered with various grasses. They receive just enough rain to sustain grass but not enough to grow many trees. Grazing animals such as antelope, giraffes, and zebra populate this biome. There are two types of grassland: savanna and temperate.

The **tundra biome** is a harsh environment located in the far north and on the tops of high mountains. There is not much precipitation, only about eight inches a year. Most of it is in the form of snow. Most of the year, the temperature in the area is below freezing. The plants of the region are mostly mosses and lichens. Animals include the Arctic fox, caribou, and polar bear.

How to Create Your Left-Hand Notebook Page

Complete the following steps to create the left-hand page of your life science notebook. Use lots of color.

Step 1: Cut out the title and glue it to the top of the notebook page.

Step 2: Cut out the puzzle flaps. Match each vocabulary word with the correct example. Apply glue to the back of each gray tab and attach the flaps below the title. Write the correct description of the biome under each flap.

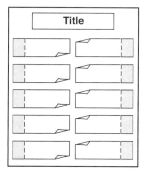

Demonstrate What You Have Learned

Choose a biome to research. Use the information to construct a diorama illustrating the distinctive kinds of plants and animals found in the biome, as well as the specific climate of the biome.

Biomes

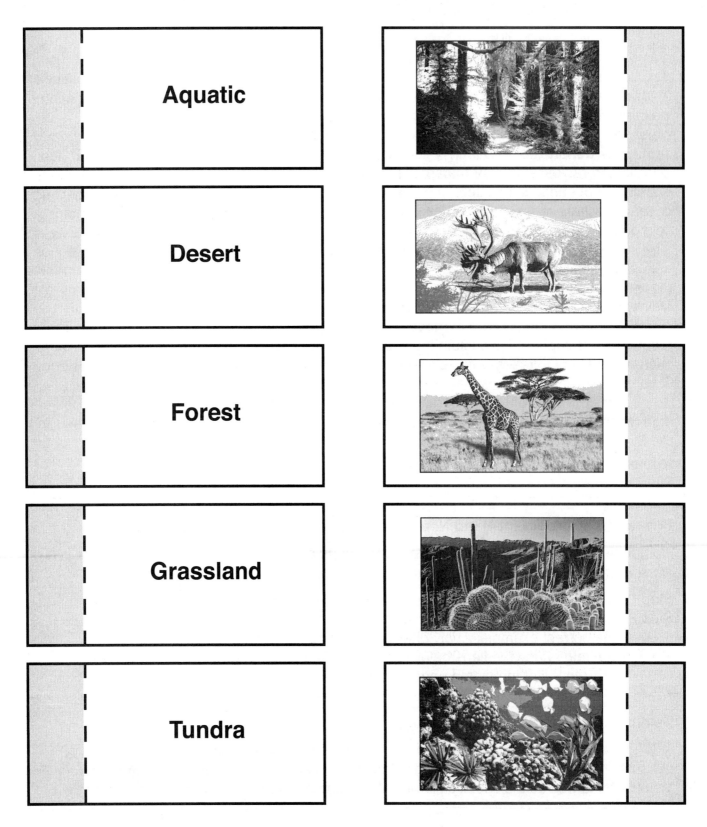

Aquatic

Desert

Forest

Grassland

Tundra

Ecosystems

Mini-Lesson

Read the following information. Then cut out and attach this box to the right-hand page of your life science notebook. Use what you have learned to create the left-hand page.

Living things can't survive alone. They live in complex ecological communities of many **species** (group of organisms that can mate and produce offspring) along with nonliving things such as water, soil, and rocks. Scientists study the many different **populations**, all the organisms of the same species, in a community.

An **ecosystem** is the combination of **biotic factors**, or living organisms, and **abiotic factors**, nonliving elements, in a given place and how they interact. Relationships in an ecosystem can be complex. Individuals within populations may compete to use the same limited resources: food, water, and space. Only those organisms that are able to get the resources they need will survive. A **habitat** is where a plant or animal lives in the ecosystem. A **niche** is the special role an organism has in the ecosystem; this includes the food it eats, type of shelter it builds, and predators that eat it. An organism's habitat and niche allow it to reduce competition for the things it needs.

Aquatic Ecosystem		
Organism	**Habitat**	**Niche**
bass	pond	eating minnows

How to Create Your Left-Hand Notebook Page

Complete the following steps to create the left-hand page of your life science notebook. Use lots of color.

Step 1: Cut out the title and glue it to the top of the notebook page.
Step 2: Cut out the flap chart. Cut on the solid line to create two vocabulary flaps. Apply glue to the back of the gray tab and attach the chart below the title. Write the correct definition under each flap.
Step 3: Cut out the second chart. Apply glue to the back and attach it at the bottom of page.
Step 4: Cut apart the picture and word cards and glue each in the correct box on the chart.

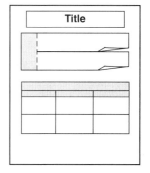

Demonstrate What You Have Learned

In your life science notebook list five organisms in a forest ecosystem. Identify each organism's habitat and niche. Use your science textbook or online sources if you need help.

Ecosystems

Ecological Communities	Species
	Population

A Garden Ecosystem

Organism	Habitat	Niche

field of clover	soil	
decomposing dead plants and animals		carrying pollen from one flower to the next

Ecosystem Cycles

Mini-Lesson

Read the following information. Then cut out and attach this box to the right-hand page of your life science notebook. Use what you have learned to create the left-hand page.

Ecological cycles are the processes by which the earth's limited resources are recycled. The recycling of resources through the biosphere (the whole area of the earth's surface, atmosphere, and sea that is inhabited by living things) keep the ecosystem functioning. Three important cycles are the water cycle, carbon-oxygen cycle, and the nitrogen cycle.

- **Water Cycle**: Water is moved in a cycle through the ecosystem in the repeated process of evaporation, condensation, and precipitation. The earth's water enters the atmosphere through **evaporation**; heat from the sun causes water on Earth to turn from liquid to gas and rise into the sky. This **water vapor** collects in the sky in the form of clouds. During **condensation**, water vapor in the clouds cools down and becomes liquid again. **Precipitation** occurs when so much water has condensed that the air cannot hold it any longer. The clouds get heavy and water falls back to the earth in the form of rain, hail, sleet, or snow.
- **Carbon-Oxygen Cycle**: Animals breathe in oxygen and breathe out carbon dioxide as a waste product. Plants need carbon dioxide. They take in carbon dioxide for photosynthesis and release oxygen as a waste product.
- **Nitrogen Cycle**: Nitrogen gas in the air is converted into nitrates by lightning. Rain and other precipitation then bring the nitrates down into the soil. Nitrogen gas in the soil is converted into nitrates by bacteria and decomposers in the soil. Plants absorb nitrates through their roots. Animals get the nitrogen compounds from the plants they eat. Animals return nitrogen compounds to the environment in their wastes. Bacteria break down the compounds and release nitrogen gas back into the atmosphere.

How to Create Your Left-Hand Notebook Page

Complete the following steps to create the left-hand page of your life science notebook. Use lots of color.

Step 1: Cut out the title and glue it to the top of the notebook page.
Step 2: Cut out the three flap charts. Apply glue to the back of each gray tab and attach the charts below the title. Write the correct definition under each flap.

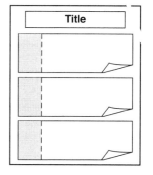

Demonstrate What You Have Learned

Construct a terrarium in order to observe the phases of the water cycle. Use your science textbook or online sources if you need help.

Ecosystem Cycles

Carbon-Oxygen Cycle

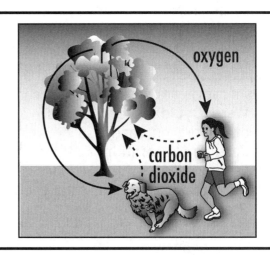

Nitrogen Cycle

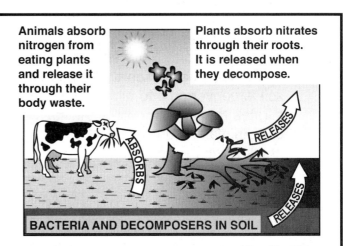

Water Cycle

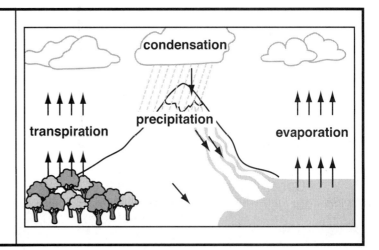

Symbiotic Relationships

Mini-Lesson

Read the following information. Then cut out and attach this box to the right-hand page of your life science notebook. Use what you have learned to create the left-hand page.

Ecosystems are very delicate and must maintain a natural balance. Organisms maintain this natural balance through symbiosis. **Symbiosis** is the relationship between two organisms. The relationship can occur within an organism's body or outside of it. There are three different types of symbiosis.

- **Commensalism** is a relationship between two kinds of organisms where one organism benefits while the other is not harmed and does not benefit. For example, the cattle egret follows water buffalo as they graze. The egrets catch and eat the insects stirred up by the water buffalo. The egret benefits, but the water buffalo does not benefit and is not harmed by the relationship.
- **Mutualism** is a relationship between two kinds of organisms that benefits both. For example, a shark depends on a cleaner fish to eat food scraps and parasites in its mouth. The cleaner fish depends on the shark for food scraps and parasites to eat. Both organisms depend on the other but are not harmed by the relationship.
- **Parasitism** is a relationship in which one organism benefits from that relationship while the other organism may be harmed by it. For example, a tick attaches to a dog to get its food (blood). The tick benefits from the relationship, but the dog is harmed. The tick bites the dog's skin, sucking its blood and causing it to itch.

How to Create Your Left-Hand Notebook Page

Complete the following steps to create the left-hand page of your life science notebook. Use lots of color.

Step 1: Cut out the title and glue it to the top of the notebook page.

Step 2: Cut out the flap chart. Apply glue to the back of the gray tab and attach it below the title. Write the correct definition under the flap.

Step 3: Cut out the puzzle pieces. Match each vocabulary word with the correct definition and example. Glue the matching pieces at the bottom of the page to create three complete arrows.

Demonstrate What You Have Learned

Copy the chart at the right in your life science notebook. Complete the chart by providing an example for each type of symbolic relationship. Use your science textbook or online sources if you need help.

Symbiotic Relationships	
Relationship	Example
mutualism	
commensalism	
parasitism	

Symbiotic Relationships

Symbiosis

| Mutualism | One organism benefits while the other organism may be harmed. | the relationship between a tick and a dog |

| Commensalism | Both organisms benefit. | the relationship between a cattle egret and a water buffalo |

| Parasitism | One organism benefits without harming or benefitting the other organism. | the relationship between a shark and a cleaner fish |

Predator-Prey Relationships

Mini-Lesson

Read the following information. Then cut out and attach this box to the right-hand page of your life science notebook. Use what you have learned to create the left-hand page.

Organisms in an ecosystem have special feeding relationships. Some animals are **predators** (kill and eat other animals for energy) and some are **prey** (animals that are killed and eaten for energy). There are many examples of predator-prey relationships: a great white shark eating a seal, a coyote eating a rabbit, or an eagle eating a fish.

Predator-prey relationships keep an ecosystem balanced by preventing any one population from getting too large. It's a cycle. When the prey species is numerous, the number of predators will increase because there is more food available. As the number of predators begins to increase, the prey population will decrease in response to the increase in the predator population. As the prey population becomes smaller, the food supply decreases, causing the predator population to decrease. This allows the prey population to increase, once again completing the cycle.

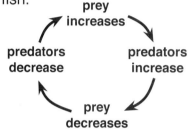

Predators and their prey evolve together. Over time, prey animals develop adaptations to help them avoid being eaten and predators develop strategies to make them more effective at catching their prey. These strategies and adaptations can take many forms, including camouflage, mimicry, defensive mechanisms, and speed. **Camouflage** allows an animal to blend in with its environment and mask its identity. An animal may **mimic**, or copy, an animal that is dangerous to a predator in order to deter an attacker. Some animals use poisons secreted from their skin to avoid being eaten. Many predators have developed the ability to move fast to capture their prey.

How to Create Your Left-Hand Notebook Page

Complete the following steps to create the left-hand page of your life science notebook. Use lots of color.

Step 1: Cut out the title and glue it to the top of the page.
Step 2: Cut out the diagram chart. Apply glue to the back of the gray tab and attach the chart below the title. Write an explanation of the predator-prey cycle under the flap.
Step 3: Cut out the flap chart. Cut on the solid line to create two flaps. Apply glue to the back of the gray tab and attach the chart at the bottom of the page. Write the correct definition under each flap.

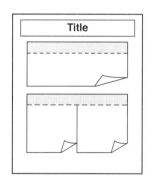

Demonstrate What You Have Learned

List five predators and their prey in your life science notebook. Use your science textbook or online sources if you need help.

Predator-Prey Relationships

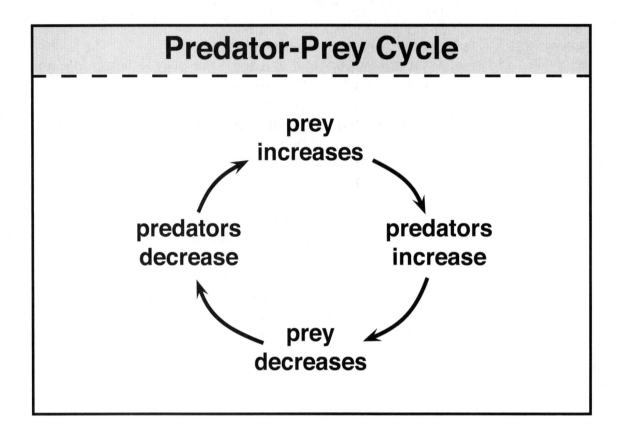

Predator-Prey Cycle

prey
increases

predators
increase

prey
decreases

predators
decrease

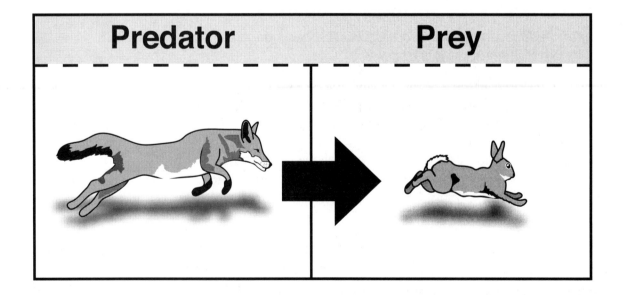

Predator	Prey

Feeding Relationships

Mini-Lesson

Read the following information. Then cut out and attach this box to the right-hand page of your life science notebook. Use what you have learned to create the left-hand page.

All living organisms need energy to live. Organisms can be divided into three main groups: producers, consumers, and decomposers. **Producers** are organisms that can make their own food: plants, algae, and bacteria. **Consumers** are organisms that get their energy by eating other organisms. **Decomposers** are organisms that get their energy from eating dead or decaying organisms.

All mammals are consumers and can be classified based on what they eat. They have specifically shaped teeth to help them eat their food.

- **Carnivores** get energy from eating other animals. They usually have sharp front incisors and long, sharp canine teeth. Grey wolves are carnivores. They hunt and eat such animals as deer, moose, and elk.
- **Omnivores** get energy from eating plants and animals. They have a variety of sharp and flat teeth because they eat a variety of foods. Raccoons are omnivores. They eat berries, nuts, and grains. They also eat insects and birds.
- **Herbivores** get energy from eating plants. They usually have large front incisors and flat, broad molars. Deer are herbivores. They eat fruits, acorns, grass, and plants.

How to Create Your Left-Hand Notebook Page

Complete the following steps to create the left-hand page of your life science notebook. Use lots of color.

Step 1: Cut out the title and glue it to the top of the notebook page.
Step 2: Cut out the flap chart. Cut on the solid lines to create six vocabulary flaps. Apply glue to the back of the gray tab and attach the chart below the title.
Step 3: Write the correct definition under each flap.

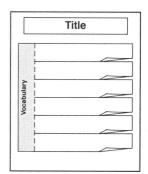

Demonstrate What You Have Learned

Observe decomposers in action. Mix sand and topsoil. Fill a glass gallon jar or transparent plastic container three-fourths full with the mixture. Add 10 to 12 red worms to the container. Place the container in a cool, dark place. Check soil often, and keep it moist but not wet. Feed the earthworms a tablespoon a week of fresh or decaying celery leaves, fruit peelings, or cornmeal. Moisten the food and put a thin layer of fresh soil over it. Throw away any food that becomes moldy or smells.

Feeding Relationships

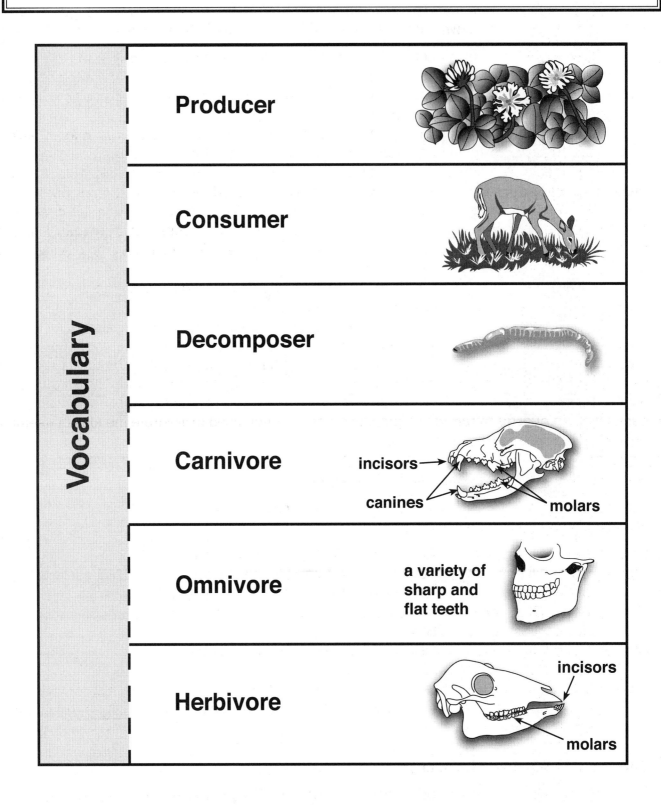

Vocabulary	
Producer	
Consumer	
Decomposer	
Carnivore	incisors → canines molars
Omnivore	a variety of sharp and flat teeth
Herbivore	incisors molars

Tracing the Flow of Energy

Mini-Lesson

Read the following information. Then cut out and attach this box to the right-hand page of your life science notebook. Use what you have learned to create the left-hand page.

All living things need energy. **Energy** originates from the sun and is transferred to animals through the food they eat. A food chain and food web are models that trace the flow of energy (food) in an ecosystem. Arrows are used to represent the direction of energy flow. They always point toward the consumer and away from the producer.

A **food chain** is a diagram of who eats what. The chain traces the energy in food back to the sun. **Producers** (plants) capture and store energy from the sun through the process of photosynthesis. A producer is the first link in a food chain. The second link is usually a **herbivore**, an organism that feeds on producers. This is called the **primary consumer**. The next links are **carnivores**, animals that eat other animals. The first carnivore in the chain is called the **secondary consumer**, a carnivore that feeds on primary consumers. The last link is the **tertiary consumer**. This is the top predator in the food chain. They can feed on producers, primary consumers, and secondary consumers.

A **food web** is a diagram of two or more food chains linked together showing how feeding relationships in an ecosystem are connected.

All living things constantly consume energy or food in order to grow and reproduce. The energy they do not use is stored. When animals eat plants and animals, the stored energy in those organisms is passed along to the consumer. Some energy is lost as heat; the rest is used for growth and reproduction. This happens all the way up the food chain. The amount of available energy at each level decreases, limiting the number of organisms that can survive at each level. An **energy pyramid** is a graphic organizer often used to illustrate the loss of useful energy at each level in the food chain.

How to Create Your Left-Hand Notebook Page

Complete the following steps to create the left-hand page of your life science notebook. Use lots of color.

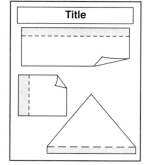

Step 1: Cut out the title and glue it to the top of the notebook page.

Step 2: Cut out the Food Chain diagram box. Apply glue to the back of the gray tab and attach it below the title. Cut out the picture cards. Glue each card in the correct box on the diagram. Write the correct definition under the flap.

Step 3: Cut out the Food Web flap chart and glue it below the diagram chart. Write the correct definition under the flap.

Step 4: Cut out the Energy Pyramid chart. Apply glue to the back of the gray tab and attach the chart at the bottom of the page. Write an explanation of how energy flows in an ecosystem under the flap.

Demonstrate What You Have Learned

In your life science notebook, draw a food chain diagram involving three consumers, with the arrows pointing in the correct direction. Label the producer and the primary, secondary, and tertiary consumers.

Tracing the Flow of Energy

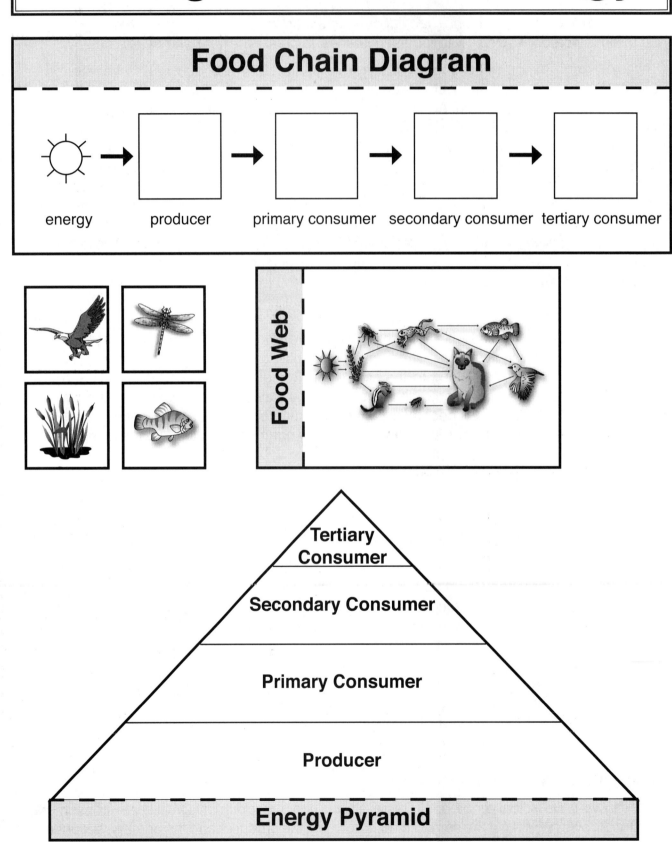

Food Chain Diagram

energy   producer   primary consumer   secondary consumer   tertiary consumer

Food Web

Tertiary Consumer

Secondary Consumer

Primary Consumer

Producer

Energy Pyramid